A MAN CALLED MIKE

Mary Mackie

Chivers Press · Thorndike Press
Bath, England · Waterville, Maine USA

This Large Print edition is published by Chivers Press, England, and by Thorndike Press, USA.

Published in 2002 in the U.K. by arrangement with the author.

Published in 2002 in the U.S. by arrangement with Juliet Burton Literary Agency.

U.K. Hardcover ISBN 0–7540–4995–7 (Chivers Large Print)
U.K. Softcover   ISBN 0–7540–4996–5 (Camden Large Print)
U.S. Softcover   ISBN 0–7862–4478–X (General Series Edition)

The text of this Large Print edition is unabridged.
Other aspects of the book may vary from the original edition.

Set in 16 pt. New Times Roman.

Printed in Great Britain on acid-free paper.

British Library Cataloguing in Publication Data available

Library of Congress Control Number: 2002105459

CHAPTER ONE

Warm in her loose-knit sweater and old jeans, Elizabeth trod carefully across the beach. Rockstrewn sand, littered with seaweed, spread out before her, with secret pools left by the tide. The thunder of waves came mutedly through a mist which cloaked the coast and hid the cliff behind her. She was absorbed in thought as she reached a familiar boulder and crouched down to see what lurked in the rockpool below.

But her mind was not on the cove, or the crabs and tiny prawns hiding among drifts of seaweed. She kept thinking about her aunt, lying pale and grief-stricken in the nursing home in St Helier. The accident had changed many things, including Elizabeth's own life. Only that morning she had had a letter from her editor at the magazine in London, telling her that her continued absence obliged him, regretfully, to terminate her employment.

Now the future looked unclear. Of course she would stay here in Jersey with Aunt Helen, who needed her. Helen had given up a good deal for Elizabeth and now it was time to repay that loyalty, even if it meant giving up her place in the flat in St John's Wood, and her social life with her friends in London. Perhaps the local paper here in the islands might have an opening for a trained journalist. At least she might, in the meantime, earn a little money freelancing.

She was so deep in thought that she failed to notice the rapid rise of the tide, filling the hollows among the rocks around her. A gull swooped out of the mist, screaming raucously, jerking her back to the present. She leapt to her feet as a fresh wave washed closer, stirring the weed in the pool. At the same moment, a dog's barking alerted her to the presence of someone else on the beach.

Out of the mist that veiled the cliff, a Great Dane bounded, bristling and barking ferociously. It rushed to stand at the edge of the rocks only a few yards from where Elizabeth stood frozen. The animal looked huge and menacing, sharp teeth showing each time it lifted its head to voice its anger.

Behind her, the sea surged, moving in to cut her off. Her only route to the sand was another sloping wedge of rocks, directly in line to where the dog waited apparently ready to tear her to pieces if she moved. She hung there, telling herself not to be so stupid, while in the back of her mind she remembered that tides in the Channel Islands rose far and swift. If she didn't soon get to the beach, her rock would be awash. But still the dog stood, barring her way, its great head thrown back as it barked so loudly that her head began to throb.

One hand holding back a swathe of honey-gold hair, she gestured at the dog. 'Shoo! Go away! Get lost, you brute!'

Then to her relief a male voice floated out of the mist, calling, 'Bran! Here, Bran!'

The dog stopped barking, though it remained alert, ears pricked and bright eyes fixed on Elizabeth's slender form. On the edge of her vision, a tall, dark figure emerged from the mist. She daren't look away from the dog. The sea foamed round her, inching higher.

'Bran!' the man said sharply. 'Come here, you great fool!'

Elizabeth let out her breath on a sigh as the animal left its stance by the rocks and padded quietly to its master's side, sleekly powerful but all obedience now.

Unfortunately, the water had risen so much that the step to the next dry rock was now a good three feet or more, demanding a leap which might send her sliding into the cold sea. Elizabeth contemplated it, gathering herself for a tricky landing.

The man stepped up on to the wedge of a rock, extending a hand. 'Allow me.'

Gratefully, with part of her mind still on the watchful dog, she reached for the proffered hand and felt herself gripped in strong fingers. He supported her as she launched herself across the gap to join him.

The rock was narrow, with barely room for both of them. In her efforts to avoid contact

3

with him, she teetered off balance, nearly pulling the man over with her. 'Steady!' he exclaimed, and his arm locked round her waist. For a second she was plastered against rippling muscle, assailed by the clean male scent of him. Flustered with embarrassment, she caught a glimpse of laughter in the bluest eyes she had ever seen.

Next moment he had leapt the short distance to the sand, where he held out his hand again. Not looking at him, she accepted his help to safety, and then she was obliged to twist free of his grasp.

'Thank you,' she muttered, one eye on the dog, which had begun to leap excitedly from side to side, barking again.

'Bran!' the man warned. 'Behave yourself!'

Bran subsided, coming to heel where his master took firm hold of a leather collar and smiled blandly at Elizabeth. 'Sorry about that.'

'You should keep him under better control,' she replied.

They made a formidable twosome, the huge dog and the tall, well-built man whose blue eyes mocked her from under a windblown fringe of dark hair. Broad shoulders filled out a traditional navy jersey, and faded jeans clung to long, long legs. From the corner of her eye, Elizabeth studied the stubborn set of his jaw and the faint curve of a chiselled mouth. Her fear of the dog seemed to amuse him.

'I'm always nervous around dogs,' she said.

4

'I've never had much to do with them.'

'He gets excited when he's out for a run,' came the reply. 'He's not very old—still got his puppy exuberance, though he won't hurt you.'

Glancing at the now-docile dog, she muttered, 'Well, if you say so.'

'Ruined your dignity, did he?'

The laughter in his voice made Elizabeth prickle with annoyance. For a long, spine-tingling moment their eyes held, his teasing, hers defiant. Something quirked in her subconscious, making her aware that as men went this one was quite a fine physical specimen.

The dog was straining towards her, held back by a big hand locked firmly in his collar. The man jerked him back, speaking sharply, and sent a sidelong glance at Elizabeth. 'Perhaps you'd better introduce yourself. To Bran, I mean. Hold out your hand—the back of it, so he can see you're not going to grab him. Let him get your scent, then if he meets you again he'll know you're a friend.'

When she hesitated, reluctant to go near either dog or man, he added drily, 'It's okay, I won't let him eat you. Not scared, are you?'

Piqued, Elizabeth edged forward, presenting the back of a clenched fist. Bran's great head strained out, his breath tickling her skin. A warm tongue caressed her with a soft touch that made her jump and withdraw her hand to wipe it on her jeans. She stepped away, relieved to be further from the tall, muscular figure of the dog's master. Momentarily, she had had the odd feeling that he might try to take hold of her. But that was irrational. She was just on edge, for some reason.

'See?' he said with satisfaction. 'Docile as a baby.'

He bent to pick up a piece of driftwood which he hurled along the beach, into the mist. Bran went loping after it.

'I'd better go,' Elizabeth said. 'I've been longer than I intended. Thanks for your help.'

'Don't mention it. Are you down here often? On holiday?'

'No, not exactly.' To her irritation, he accompanied her as she moved towards the cliff, which loomed darkly through the mist; then the dog reappeared, bounding towards her like a young lion intent on boisterous play. Elizabeth stopped, but Bran only leapt round her a couple of times before loping off for the cliff path. He paused and looked back, woofing as if inviting her to follow.

'Looks as though you've made a conquest,' the man said with a grin. 'We'll go up together, shall we? It's a pretty steep climb. Don't want you falling.'

'I'm not completely helpless,' she retorted.

'Oh, I'm sure you're not,' he said, but his smile said otherwise, infuriating her.

Gritting her teeth, she went after the dog, which bounded agilely up the steep, uneven

6

path. The man followed her, so she was caught between them, and once her foot did slip and a steadying hand in the small of her back saved her from a minor disaster. Feeling unutterably stupid, Elizabeth clambered on, reaching the top out of breath.

On the headland, a martello tower, relic of old wars with France, lifted its rounded sides up into the mist. Elizabeth followed the path across the clifftop, among gorse bushes brilliant with yellow flowers. The path sloped down, coming eventually into open woodland where the mist was less dense.

The man stayed with her, while Bran ran back and forth investigating tree roots and returning to dance circles round his master. Elizabeth was relieved to see the fork in the path, one branch heading down to the road while the other turned aside to a gate in a fence—the fence round Belle Mer, her aunt's luxurious home.

She stopped at the fork, throwing her hair back over her shoulder in a nonchalant gesture designed to disguise her agitation. "Bye, then.'

The man glanced at the gate, then at her, his eyes narrowing. 'You're from Belle Mer?'

'I'm staying there, yes. Something wrong with that?'

His teasing manner had gone, wiped away by a coldness that puzzled her. With deliberate insolence, he looked her up and down, his eyes seeming to probe through her clothes to the naked curves beneath. After an interval that made her cheeks burn and her eyes blaze with sea-green fire, he looked at her face.

'How's Mrs Sorensen?'

'Still very ill,' Elizabeth replied. 'How did you know—'

'Everybody knows,' he cut in. 'Ben Sorensen had become quite well known here, for all he was an incomer. Millionaires don't stay anonymous when they get themselves killed the way he did. Flying his own plane, wasn't he? Killed himself and badly injured his wife?'

'That's right,' she said stiffly, annoyed by the careless way he spoke of the tragedy. 'Not that it's any concern of yours, Mr . . .'

'My friends call me Mike,' he informed her.

'How nice for them,' Elizabeth clipped. 'Now, if you'll excuse me . . .'

As she moved away, his hand on her arm stopped her and when she glanced round he said casually, 'Are you busy tonight?'

She regarded him in astonishment, but his eyes were opaque, telling her nothing. She must have misheard. 'Sorry?'

'I asked if you were doing anything tonight,' he said evenly. 'I thought we might have dinner, get better acquainted. You must be bored on your own at Belle Mer.'

Thoroughly unnerved, Elizabeth eased free of his grasp, beginning to understand why Ben Sorensen had warned her about strangers. But then Ben had seen kidnappers and fortune-

8

hunters under every bush. His wealth had made him paranoid about security.

'I visit Mrs Sorensen every evening,' she said.

'*Every* evening?'

'Without fail,' she replied. 'And even if I didn't . . .'

'You're much too good for the likes of me,' he ended for her.

She ventured a glance at his carved-oak expression. Those blue eyes might have come straight out of deep-freeze for all the warmth they contained. 'That isn't what I meant. It's just . . . I don't know you. Two minutes' acquaintance on a beach is hardly enough to—'

'That's not what I heard,' he said.

Green eyes wide in a face gone pale, Elizabeth backed away. 'I *beg* your pardon?'

'You know, you do that "injured innocent" bit very well,' he commented with a cynical twist of his lips. 'I might find it almost convincing if I didn't know better. Unfortunately, I know all about you, Miss Sorensen.'

Comprehension flooded through her. He had mistaken her for Ben's daughter, obviously. She lifted her chin, staring him in the eye. 'My name isn't Sorensen.'

'Oh, of course.' A soft step brought him closer and she backed away again, mesmerised by blue eyes glinting with chill dislike. 'I forgot—you're married. Or is it divorced?' Without warning, he grabbed her left hand, bruising it between hard fingers. 'You're not wearing a ring, I see.'

'Please!' Her bones felt to be splintering as she tried to tug free, then a cry of alarm escaped her as his arm closed round her waist, pulling her full against him. His other hand curved up her back to her neck and a thumb beneath her jaw forced her to lift her face. Through eyes misted by fear, she saw his lips curl in an unpleasant smile as he lifted his body more closely to hers.

'Why, what's wrong?' he asked in a whisper that thrummed along her taut nerves. 'I thought you enjoyed being irresistible.'

His head came down and she clamped her lips tight as he kissed her with punishing force. His mouth felt hot and wet, with sharp teeth that grazed her skin. She twisted in frantic revulsion and he released her so abruptly that she stumbled sideways into a tree and huddled there, breathless with horror.

'Well, here's one man who isn't about to fall at your feet,' he said with disgust. 'I wouldn't want you if you were served up on a silver platter. With or without your inheritance!'

A rush of tears flooded her eyes as she straightened herself, hating him. With as much dignity as she could muster, she croaked, 'I don't have any inheritance. My name is Elizabeth Page. Mrs Sorensen is my aunt!'

Without waiting for his reaction, she darted for the gate. Behind her, he shouted, 'Wait!

Wait, please!'

The latch clicked up and she was inside the grounds, turning to close the gate as her tormentor strode up on the other side, his face twisted with remorse.

'I'm sorry!' he said forcefully. 'Why didn't you say?'

'Why didn't you ask?' Elizabeth cried. 'Oh, go away. Go away before I call the police!'

She fled, down through woods where daffodils nodded amid a tangle of ivy and brambles. The path came out on a sloping lawn with Belle Mer a white sprawling shape through the mist. It had broad windows and balconies, a verandah, flower-beds, and a patio outside the flat-roofed extension which held the swimming pool. She ran all the way to the verandah and opened big sliding doors into the lounging area, all deep blues and greens with touches of acid yellow in the lamps.

In the middle of the big room she stopped, gasping for breath, wiping her hand across her mouth in an effort to erase the feel of arrogant, hurtful lips. But she couldn't erase the memory, or the painful knowledge that, until he turned nasty, he had seemed the most attractive man she had ever met.

'Miss Page?' The voice made her turn to see the short, slim figure of Finch, the butler. 'Is everything all right, Miss Page?'

'Yes!' she replied breathlessly. 'I've been running. What is it, Finch?'

'Mrs Finch would like to know if you would care for apple sauce or redcurrant jelly with your pork this evening.'

The triviality of his question struck her as incongruous just at that moment. 'Oh . . . redcurrant jelly, I think.'

'I'll tell her,' said Finch, withdrawing to the kitchen where his wife held sway as cook and housekeeper.

Elizabeth dined in lonely splendour, as she had done since she came to Jersey a few weeks before. The meal was served by Finch—he and his wife headed a casual staff of cleaners and gardeners—and the food was delicious, as always. Unfortunately, Elizabeth's appetite had been sparrow-sized lately. She hated to eat alone, she was worried about her aunt, and the future hung in front of her obscured by dark cloud. Many times she wished she was back at the flat making scrambled eggs for Lu and Bettina, her flatmates, with Ben Sorensen still alive and his wife in good health.

But that was not to be. Things were as they were and her aunt needed her. It was intolerable that a man who called himself Mike should have added his own unpleasantness to an already unhappy situation.

*   *   *

Later, she drove through mist-haunted lanes to St Helier, to the nursing home where her aunt was being cared for.

'She's a bit tired,' the nurse on duty warned Elizabeth. 'I found her weeping after you left this afternoon. It's only natural she should be depressed, but Dr James is concerned about her state of mind. She's got to want to get well again.'

'You think she doesn't?' Elizabeth asked, gripped by sudden fear.

'I think she hasn't yet made up her mind. It happens sometimes. She'll never be entirely fit again—she knows that. She's going to need a great deal of care and consideration if she's ever to get back to anything like a normal life. At the moment, she's wondering if it's worth the effort. We've got to convince her that it is.'

The doctor had said much the same, on several occasions. From now on, Helen Sorensen must be protected from shocks and upheavals, or she might slip back over the edge simply because she didn't have the strength to carry on.

'I'll do my best,' said Elizabeth. 'She does have reasons to live. She has me, and her friends, and her home.'

The nurse smiled. 'Just try to make *her* see that.'

Helen Sorensen looked frail in the big bed with a cage humped over her plastered leg. Her usually well-tended fair hair was lank, her face wan. The toll of injuries made her look much older than her forty-two years. Deep shadows bruised beneath eyes that had lost their sparkle. But, as usual, Helen raised a bright smile which didn't fool Elizabeth for a minute.

'Hello, love. Here again? It must be a bore for you having to come twice a day.'

'It isn't a bore at all,' Elizabeth denied. 'I like to see you. Besides, I'd rather be here than sitting on my own at Belle Mer.'

'You should go out more,' her aunt said. 'I'm sure Nathan Frazer would be only too pleased to take you out for an evening. He's such a nice man.'

'So you keep telling me.' With a wry smile, Elizabeth drew a chair near to the bed and sat down. 'All right, if you insist, perhaps I will ask Nathan for a date. After all, we're supposed to be liberated now.'

'That's what they say,' Helen smiled. 'But where Nathan's concerned all you need do is drop a hint and he'll pick it up like a shot. I know he's very fond of you. I've seen the way he watches you when he comes here— supposedly to visit me. He's shy, that's all. And he's been very good since Ben . . .' Her sentence faltered and suddenly the empty grief was back in her eyes.

'Well, we'll see,' Elizabeth said quietly. 'But I don't want him to think I'm encouraging him. I like Nathan, but there's nothing special between us.'

With an effort, Helen pulled back from the

brink of tears. 'Then you ought to find someone who *is* special. You need something to think about, apart from me.'

'Which means a man?' Elizabeth asked. 'Aunt Helen, there are lots more interesting things in life than men.'

Helen sighed. 'That sounds like a direct quote from me, before I met Ben. You're almost twenty-four, Elizabeth. A career can be very sterile if it's all you have. You know, you're looking pale this evening. Are you tired?'

'A bit, maybe.'

'You're losing weight,' her aunt observed.

'I'm on a diet,' Elizabeth lied. 'It's fashionable to be thin these days.'

The conversation had taken her mind back to the man on the beach. He had not made her feel anything but threatened, but at least he had reminded her what it felt like to be totally alive, with all her senses working at full rate. The memory disturbed her, not only because of the anger she had sensed in him. Even now her flesh remembered the contact of his body, and his image was clear in her mind, snapping blue eyes and that well-shaped mouth drawn into a grim line.

She glanced at her left hand and saw the beginnings of bruises where his fingers had pressed flesh against bone. He had certainly left a deep impression on her, in more ways than one!

'How are *you* feeling this evening?' she asked her aunt.

'A little tired,' Helen admitted, and her eyes filled again with tears. 'I keep thinking about Ben. I still can't entirely believe I'll never see him again. I loved him, Elizabeth. That sort of emotion isn't reserved only for the young, you know. In his way, he was good to me. You must let me grieve.'

She groped for the box of tissues on the cabinet, mopping her tears while Elizabeth sat silent, thinking about the debt she owed to her aunt.

Her mother had died when Elizabeth was small, and since her father's work often took him away he had left his little daughter in the care of her grandmother and her aunt, who was then in her early twenties. Gran had kept house while Helen worked to support them all, giving up her chances of marriage since no man seemed to want to take on the responsibility for an ailing old lady and someone else's child.

Eventually, Elizabeth's father had remarried, but his new wife refused to take his daughter, too, and gradually he faded from Elizabeth's life. Her grandmother died, leaving her with Helen, who by that time had turned thirty and saw herself as a perennial spinster. She devoted herself to Elizabeth despite the inevitable battles as Elizabeth passed through her teens and started out on her journalistic

16

career, which eventually took her to London.

And then, when Helen had given up hope of finding a husband, she took a holiday in Jersey and met the wealthy Ben Sorensen, a man in his fifties but still handsome and virile. Elizabeth had been delighted when the pair married and settled at Belle Mer in seeming bliss.

The only drawback had been Ben's possessive daughter, Gayle, who had resented her stepmother. But fortunately Gayle was married to an American and lived in the States, so Helen was not often subject to her vitriol. Helen had been happy, as Elizabeth had seen when she visited Jersey. She had adored her husband, loved her home, and looked forward to many years of contentment.

Now, three years later, her happiness was ended. When Helen and Ben were returning from a holiday at their villa in Naples, their plane had crashed. Ben was killed outright, his wife critically injured. A phone call from Nathan Frazer had summoned Elizabeth to come, to offer what comfort she could.

Sometimes she thought that her presence must be scant consolation for what Helen had lost.

'How are things at Belle Mer?' Helen asked. 'Are my hyacinths out yet?'

'They're just showing some colour,' Elizabeth replied. 'You might be home while they're still in bloom. Everything else is fine.

17

Finch and his wife send their regards, as always. They'll be glad when you're home—they're bored with only me to look after. And to be honest, I feel a bit of a fraud. I'm not used to being waited on. I've been writing a few articles just to make myself feel useful, though I haven't yet heard if any have been accepted.'

'I keep telling you,' Helen sighed, 'there's no need for you to stay here, love. Don't fret about me. Your life's in London—your friends, and your job.'

'Not any more,' said Elizabeth, recalling the letter which had come that morning with a cheque in lieu of notice, though she couldn't tell Helen she had been sacked or Helen would feel responsible for it. 'I'm resigning from the magazine. I'll try freelancing for a while, and maybe try for a job on the *Jersey Evening Post*. If I have to start from the bottom again it won't matter.'

More tears glazed Helen's eyes. 'It's so much to ask of you.'

'You're not asking,' Elizabeth pointed out. 'I'm deciding for myself. Even when you're well again, you won't want to be alone. Besides, I like it here. It's not so frenetic as London. And really, there's no one I'm desperately missing. Bettina writes occasionally, so I keep up with the news.'

'Have you heard from Gayle?' asked Helen.

Elizabeth shook her head. 'You don't really

expect her to communicate with us, do you? She'll be sitting back waiting to hear how rich she'll be when the lawyers have cleared everything up.'

'Don't sound so bitter,' Helen pleaded, her thin hand moving across the counterpane until Elizabeth took it and warmed it between her own. 'I always knew that Ben intended to leave everything to Gayle. We just didn't expect it to happen so soon. I've got enough money to live on, and Gayle did say I could stay at Belle Mer as long as I wished.'

'Magnanimous of her,' Elizabeth murmured. 'I wonder how she'll react to *my* staying there, too? She only has three other homes. She'll probably charge me board and lodgings.'

'Don't be silly, of course she won't. I'm sure Ben will have made provision for me to stay at Belle Mer while I live. That's all I want—just to stay put where I was happy with him. I know you don't like Gayle much, but—'

'I only dislike her because of her attitude to you,' Elizabeth argued. 'After all, I've only met her briefly a couple of times. But even then it was clear she was jealous of you. She thought you were a fortune-hunter. *You*!'

'It can't have been easy for her,' Helen said reasonably. 'She lost her own mother, and then there were two other stepmothers before me, who both took as much as they could when they divorced Ben. Gayle hasn't had an easy life. And now her own marriage has ended in

19

disaster. When she came over here last year—when her divorce was pending—she was terribly unhappy.'

Remembering a hard mouth which had crushed and bruised hers, Elizabeth asked, 'What did she do with herself when she was here?'

'I'm not sure,' Helen sighed. 'I didn't see much of her. She was restless, poor girl. Ben provided her with a car and most of the time she was out somewhere. I suppose she made friends, but she never confided in me. I tried to talk to her, as I've tried to talk to you when you've had problems. But Gayle won't let me get near her.'

Elizabeth found it hard to be as charitable towards Gayle as her aunt was. To her mind, Gayle was wilful and selfish, used to having her own way. It didn't take much imagination to guess how she had spent her time in Jersey last year: she was blonde and beautiful, besides being wealthy. She attracted men like wasps round a honey-pot.

But quite where the man on the beach came into it, and why he had taken it upon himself to teach a lesson in humility to a girl he had never met, was a mystery.

CHAPTER TWO

Elizabeth tried to put the man named Mike out of her mind, but the memory of her encounter with him continued to haunt her. As a result, she stayed away from the lonely cove, fearing another meeting.

Instead, when she went walking she usually made for the other side of the headland, where the martello tower looked down on the shallow curve of a bay where a village clustered among trees. Once the place had earned its living from the sea, but now only a couple of fishing boats plied to and from the stone jetty and the harbour was mostly used by pleasure craft. Two concrete runways leading down the beach served as a witness to the old trade of seaweed gathering, when islanders would haul carts down to the shore to bring back vraic for fertiliser.

On Sunday morning, Elizabeth wandered along the quayside. Early holidaymakers and local children enjoyed the air on the beach and two yachts lay at anchor on the rippling tide, with a couple of smaller boats tacking further out to sea. Outside the Old Bosun Inn, big bright sunshades spread over round tables.

Elizabeth leaned on the quayside rail, smiling at the clutch of children who waited on the waterline to jump back from the next wave.

21

On clear golden air, seagulls sailed effortlessly, and now and then a voice came on the breeze from one of the boats.

A dinghy with an orange sail was making for the beach, with a redheaded girl at the tiller while a man brought down the sail. Just as the sail dropped, Elizabeth's pulses jumped as she recognised the tall, life-jacketed figure with tousled dark hair—it was the man who called himself Mike.

Fortunately he was twenty yards from her and too busy bringing the boat safely aground to take much notice of his surroundings. Elizabeth watched as he leapt lithely into the shallows and tethered the rope to a buoy before lending a hand to his companion. He caught her round her slim waist and hoisted her to dry ground, where she laughed up at him in delight. She was awfully young, Elizabeth thought with a curious lurch of disapproval. Or was it dismay?

A tawny whirlwind streaked past her, and Bran launched himself down the steps to rush and greet his master. Laughing, Mike accepted the dog's ecstatic welcome, lifting his face away from Bran's eager tongue, and then Bran went wagging round the redhead receiving more gestures of affection.

Suddenly Mike swung round to stare across the separating yards to where Elizabeth stood, as though he had noticed her presence before but had only just registered her identity.

22

'Elizabeth!' he shouted, starting towards her.

For no reason at all, she panicked, turned and hurried away.

'Elizabeth!' he yelled behind her. She broke into a run, dodging past curious people on the quay, making for the wooded road which would take her back to Belle Mer. She glanced round once, to see Mike striding in pursuit, and then she fled as if he were Satan, her heart pounding in her throat.

At last she reached the shelter of trees that would hide her. The road wound up the hillside. She ran on until her legs were shaking and she had to stop for breath. Behind her, the road was empty. Mike had given up the chase.

Damn the man! she thought viciously, furious with herself. Why on earth had she run like a scared rabbit? She was sweating profusely, all her muscles shaking. What was wrong with her? Was it fear that made her react so violently to him? She didn't understand herself, but one thing was for sure—from now on she would avoid the bay as well as the cove, though if this went on he would manage to put the whole island out of bounds for her.

*   *   *

A few days later, after more visits to the hospital, where Helen was making very slow progress towards recovery, Elizabeth received a letter. It came from someone who signed himself J-M Delaval, and informed Elizabeth that he wished to discuss a matter of business concerning her and her aunt. Perhaps she would ring his secretary and fix a suitable time?

Puzzled, Elizabeth examined the heading on the notepaper, which bore the legend 'Delaval (Channel Islands) Ltd' and had an address of one of the big hotels in St Helier. As Finch came to clear the breakfast table, Elizabeth asked him if he knew anything about a Mr Delaval.

Finch shook his head, his face expressionless as ever. 'I've only heard the name, miss. The Delaval family have a finger in many pies.'

'Did Mr Sorensen do business with them?' she asked.

'He may have done,' Finch replied. 'Perhaps Mr Frazer could help you.'

'Yes, perhaps he could,' Elizabeth agreed thoughtfully, tapping the letter against a long thumbnail. Naturally Finch didn't know anything, or if he did he wouldn't be indiscreet enough to say so. He had been well trained in the art of playing blind and deaf.

However, the mystery of the letter might be explained by a visit to Nathan Frazer, who managed the car-hire business which Ben had owned. She had first met Nathan on her visits to Helen and Ben; then after the accident he had phoned and brought her hurrying from

24

London. He had met her at the airport, stood beside her through the funeral, done everything he could to help her during those first bewildering days. And then he had slowly withdrawn, telling her to contact him if she needed him. Lately she had seen him only when he called at the nursing home to bring flowers to her aunt.

Elizabeth knew very well why Nathan kept away from her: he would have liked their relationship to develop beyond friendship. Receiving no reciprocal signals from her, however, he had said nothing, only put distance between them to allow her space and time. Which was sweet of him, Elizabeth thought, but it also made her reluctant to ask for his help, because she didn't feel anything for him but the warmest regard. Nathan was a nice man, as her aunt kept telling her, but for Elizabeth 'nice' wasn't nearly enough.

The letter from J-M Delaval bothered her. He said the matter was important and urgent, but what business could involve him with her and her aunt?

Waiting until office hours, she telephoned the number on the letter and found herself speaking to a woman with a husky French accent.

'No, I regret Mr Delaval is not available at the moment,' the secretary said. 'Shall I ask him to call back? Who's speaking, please?'

'My name is Elizabeth Page. I had a letter—'

'Oh, yes!' the woman interrupted. 'Miss Page, of course. Yes, I was told you might call. Mr Delaval wonders if you'd be kind enough to have dinner with him one evening.'

'Dinner?' Elizabeth queried. 'I understood it was a business matter.'

'Yes, but I believe it's something he'd rather discuss informally with you over a meal. He suggests Friday evening, if that's convenient for you.'

Frowning to herself, Elizabeth puzzled over this unexpected invitation. She had nothing to do on Friday, apart from visiting her aunt, but Helen did keep saying she ought to go out socially and not feel bound to twice-daily trips to the nursing home. Besides, if it was important, perhaps she ought to accept.

'Can you give me some idea why Mr Delaval wants to see me?' she asked.

'He did not say,' the voice purred. 'Will Friday suit you? Mr Delaval suggests that The Cliff restaurant has an excellent cuisine. If you could be there at eight o'clock, that will fit into his schedule nicely.'

Mr Delaval's 'suggestions' sounded more like royal commands. Every word worried Elizabeth more. He sounded to be an extremely important and busy man, yet he wanted to buy her dinner. What on earth did it mean?

'I'll be there,' she replied. 'Friday evening, eight o'clock, at The Cliff.'

26

'That's correct. It's in St Fleur, above the harbour. I'm sure Mr Delaval will be delighted you were able to accept. Thank you for calling, Miss Page. Goodbye.'

Thoroughly intrigued now, Elizabeth drove over to the airport, where Nathan Frazer had his office tucked behind the car-hire reception. She was shown into the manager's office, where Nathan rose smiling from behind his desk to offer her a seat.

'This is a pleasant surprise,' he said warmly. 'I hope there's nothing wrong.'

'No, not really,' Elizabeth sighed. 'I just wanted to pick your brains about something. This letter came this morning.'

He perched on his desk to read it, light catching on his steel-rimmed glasses. He was a lean, rangy man of about forty, immaculately dressed in suit and tie, with his chestnut hair cut short. Freckles sprinkled his pleasant features, giving him a homely look. He was attractive; Elizabeth could see that, but for her he struck no sparks. He was just dear, nice Nathan, on whom she could rely.

Having read the letter twice, he remained for a moment with his head bent, rubbing his chin thoughtfully before glancing to where Elizabeth sat waiting for his verdict.

'Well?' she prompted impatiently. 'Does it ring any bells with you?'

Nathan shook his head, slowly handing the letter back to her. 'I know the name,' he said,

27

folding his hands in his lap. 'Everyone in the islands knows the name Delaval. They have interests all over the place, here, in France and elsewhere. I assume the Delaval in question is Jean-Michel, who's managing director of their island companies. But why he should want to see you . . . I've really no idea.'

Sighing, Elizabeth stared at the paper in her hand. 'It must have something to do with Ben, I suppose.'

'Probably,' said Nathan in a dour tone that made her lift her head sharply. He slid off the desk and went to stand by the window looking across the airport car park. 'I know Ben crossed swords with the Delavals a few times. He tried to buy his way in here and there around the islands, but the established businessmen—particularly the Delavals— regarded him as a Johnny-come-lately. There are a lot of rich men here, so his wealth didn't impress him. And, as you know, he was inclined to behave like a bull in a china shop. His manner wasn't calculated to make people like him.'

'I know. But that doesn't explain—'

'All I can think,' Nathan interrupted, coming to stand in front of her, 'is that it has something to do with Belle Mer. It belonged to the Delavals before Ben acquired it. Perhaps they want it back.'

Elizabeth shot to her feet, appalled. 'Well, they can't have it! You don't think Gayle would sell it, do you? Nathan, it's the only home my aunt has!'

'I only said perhaps,' he reminded her, laying calming hands on her shoulders. A second later, he seemed to realise that he shouldn't be touching her. He removed his hands and stepped away, going to sit behind his desk, saying casually, 'How is your aunt, by the way?'

'A bit better.' Her face twisted. She wanted to apologise to him for being unable to return his feelings, but the subject had never been raised openly between them and now was hardly the time. 'The doctors have warned me she'll have to take things easy. She won't be an invalid, exactly, but she'll need care, and a quiet life.'

He looked at her over the top of his glasses, calm grey eyes fringed with thick pale lashes. 'Will you be staying here, then?'

'Yes, I plan to.' Restless, she turned away, then turned back again. 'Nathan, you don't really think the Delavals want Belle Mer, do you? Sometimes I think it's only the thought of going back home that's keeping Aunt Helen going. She loves that house, and the garden. She's taken three years getting it the way she wants it. Her happiest memories are there.'

'And she has the right to live there for the rest of her life, I understand.'

Rubbing a finger along his shining desk, Elizabeth let her shoulders slump and pulled a wry face. 'That's what she says. I just hope Mr

Delaval's not the persistent sort. He probably spends his days making high-powered business deals. If he makes Gayle an offer, she may sell the place just to spite Aunt Helen.'

'If his reputation is anything to go by . . .' Nathan began meaningfully, and spread his hands. 'I could be totally wrong. It could be nothing to do with Belle Mer. Unless, of course, Ben has left the house to your aunt after all.'

'She thinks that's unlikely,' said Elizabeth, dropping back into the chair. 'What did you mean about Mr Delaval's reputation?'

In the precise, thoughtful way that he had, which irritated her beyond reason, Nathan made a tent with his hands, tapping his fingers against his lips as he considered what to say. 'If what people say is true, Jean-Michel Delaval is a tough cookie. He's been working abroad, overseeing the family's interests in foreign parts, I understand. When his grandfather died last year, Jean-Michel came back and took over as big boss of their Channel Island operations. Hotels, restaurants, horticulture . . . You name it, they're involved in it.'

'I see,' Elizabeth said, perplexed. 'Then why is he taking me to dinner?'

Nathan flinched visibly. 'Dinner? I assumed you'd be seeing him at his office.'

'No, when I phoned the secretary she said he preferred an informal meeting. So I'm having dinner with him on Friday night. At

The Cliff.'

'Well, where else?' Nathan said cynically. 'He can afford to take you to the most exclusive restaurant on the island, especially since his company owns the place. Are you going to tell your aunt about it?'

'I shall have to. It will mean missing my visit to her that evening.'

'Then play it down,' Nathan advised. 'No need to worry her unnecessarily.'

'I shan't,' she said. 'If she thought anything was going to happen to Belle Mer she'd go crazy. But you're right—if it was about the house, he wouldn't be wanting to talk to me. So he must have some other reason. It's probably nothing to worry about at all. Thank you, Nathan—I knew talking to you would be a help.'

He smiled, but his eyes were mournful as a puppy's. 'What are friends for? If you like, I'll stand in for you at the nursing home on Friday night. It's horrible lying in bed, in pain, knowing it's visiting time and having no one come to see you.'

'You're awfully kind,' she said gratefully, rising to leave.

He, too, came to his feet, walking to the door where he paused with his hand on the knob, head on one side as he looked down into her face. 'Any time, Elizabeth. If there's anything I can do, or if you just want to talk to somebody, I'm here. By the way, I don't suppose you've heard from the lawyers yet, have you?'

'Ben's lawyers? No, not yet. They did say it would take some time—Ben's affairs were complicated. Why?'

'Oh, I just wondered. I've been looking into the possibility of buying Sorensen Car Hire. I don't suppose Gayle will want to be bothered with it and it would be nice to be working for myself. I could manage it, with a bank loan to start off with.'

'Then I wish you luck,' Elizabeth replied with a smile. 'But, talking about Gayle . . . I suppose you must have met her when she was over here last year.'

'I did,' Nathan agreed, his expression suddenly guarded.

'Did she . . . socialise a lot?'

Curiously, the question seemed to make him uncomfortable. A dull flush crept up his cheeks.

'It depends what you mean,' he hedged.

'You know very well what I mean! Gayle is a social animal. She's beautiful, rich, sexy.'

His flush darkened, his eyes sliding from hers. 'If you're asking me if I took her out— yes, I did. And I wasn't the only one.'

Belatedly, she understood the reasons for his discomfort. Nathan must have fallen victim to Gayle's all-too-obvious allure, though Elizabeth had never dreamed of such a thing.

She laid a hand on his sleeve, saying softly,

32

'Oh, Nathan . . . You fell for her?'

'I was a bloody fool!' he said fiercely. 'I hoped you'd never find out. Did your aunt tell you?'

'No.' She wished she had never raised the subject. 'As a matter of fact, the thought had never crossed my mind. I only asked because . . . well, it's not important. You've told me what I wanted to know. I'm sorry if I embarrassed you. I didn't intend to.'

He looked so wretched that she reached impulsively to kiss his cheek and swiftly drew away again, saying, 'Don't look like that. She's not worth it—really she's not.'

'It's not *her* that—' he began, and stopped himself, opening the door for her. 'Goodbye, Elizabeth. And good luck for your meeting with Delaval.'

She went out into the fresh air, thinking that one could never tell about people. Who would have dreamed that Gayle would draw poor Nathan into her net, however briefly? He hadn't stood a chance with a man-eater like Gayle. But Elizabeth was sorry to have caused him distress.

Actually, she hadn't been thinking about Nathan at all: her mind had been back on a grim-lipped man who for some unaccountable reason had taken *her* for Gayle Sorensen.

*   *   *

33

As Nathan had advised, she was very careful not to say too much about her dinner engagement when next she saw her aunt. Helen seemed delighted that Elizabeth had a date, and she didn't press too hard for details after Elizabeth promised to tell her all about it on Saturday.

'I'm only sorry it's not Nathan,' Helen commented. 'There he is dying for a kind word from you, and you go off and have dinner with some handsome stranger! He *is* handsome, I suppose?'

'Devastating,' Elizabeth said, tongue in cheek.

'But where did you meet him?'

'Oh, around—you know. Aunt Helen, you promised not to ask questions. I'll be here on Saturday and then I swear I'll tell you every last detail.'

Helen laughed, pretending to look coy. 'You don't have to go *that* far, love! Just the gist will do.'

Clearly she thought Elizabeth had made a conquest, but the deception served its pupose. Until Elizabeth discovered just what Jean-Michel Delaval had in mind, Helen might as well indulge herself imagining a romantic encounter for her niece.

*   *   *

On Friday evening, Elizabeth groomed herself

carefully, pinning her hair up in a sophisticated style which showed off its sun-gold highlights. She chose a scoop-necked dress in a silky green clinging fabric shot with gold, and she dressed it up with a plain gold necklet and ear-rings. The result looked suitable for The Cliff and she hoped it would not disgrace her wealthy escort. She wished she knew more about him. Was he young, old, married, single, fat, thin?

Taking her aunt's white Granada, as usual, she drove across the island to where in a pretty bay the village of St Fleur lay on sloping streets leading down to a harbour. On one headland, a mediaeval castle towered against the evening sky, and on the other a road twined up beneath a tunnel of trees to the stepped car parks below the long, low building which held The Cliff restaurant.

At exactly eight o'clock, Elizabeth stepped into a deep-carpeted foyer where arched openings led off to various bars and into the restaurant itself. She glanced round at other people arriving, wondering if one of them could be Jean-Michel Delaval. But all the men had companions and some were in groups, drifting through to the bars laughing and chattering. Eventually, Elizabeth approached a girl who sat behind a tiny reception desk.

'Excuse me. I'm supposed to be meeting Mr Delaval.'

The girl looked up, giving Elizabeth an appraising glance. 'Oh—yes.' She picked up her phone. 'He's in conference with the manager. I'll tell him you're here.'

Feeling nervous, Elizabeth strolled to plate glass windows draped in net, overlooking the car parks where all the time more vehicles were arriving beneath a sky beginning to be coloured with sunset. She wondered if the boss of Delaval (Channel Islands) Ltd. was given to meeting strange young women in his own restaurants.

She kept glancing behind her as people moved to and from the bars and the dining room, until she saw a man emerge from the office behind the reception desk—a man in immaculate dinner jacket and black bow tie, tall and dark . . .

Oh, it couldn't be!

She seemed to stop breathing. The world swayed and a grey mist threatened to claim her. All she could clearly see was that tanned, familiar face with blue eyes gleaming sardonically as he made his way among the people in the foyer, coming directly to where she stood.

'Good evening,' said the man who called himself Mike.

'What are you doing here?' Elizabeth got out in a strangled voice.

A dark eyebrow quirked slightly, but otherwise his face remained bland, his eyes steady on hers. 'I'm taking you to dinner, aren't I?'

'You're not—'

'I'm afraid I am,' he said evenly.

'But—' She glanced around the foyer, deciding it was not the place to create a scene. He had trapped her very neatly, even placing himself between her and the door.

She took refuge in icy disdain, facing him with blazing eyes. 'You're Jean-Michel Delaval?'

'I am.'

'Then it was a trick!'

He made a pained face. 'Oh, hardly a trick. Be honest—if I'd invited you out any other way, would you have come? After the way you ran away from me last Sunday at the harbour I gathered you wouldn't meet me if I declared myself openly. I . . . I've brought you some flowers.' A glance drew her attention to the clear plastic box in his hands, where a spray of bright orchids nestled. 'I owe you an apology, I believe.'

'Fine.' She accepted the flowers reluctantly, furious at the spot he had put her in. 'And now that we've got that over, perhaps you'll allow me to leave.'

'No.' His hand closed round her bare arm as she tried to edge past him. He moved round her, backing her into a corner where his tall frame hid her from most other people in the foyer. 'We're having dinner. It's the least I can do.'

'The least you can do is let me go!' she

37

hissed, feeling threatened by his proximity. His sheer maleness was almost overpowering, every tall, lithe, athletic inch of him impinging itself on her senses.

'You don't mean that,' he told her.

'I do mean it!' she flung at him in a charged undertone. 'You inveigled me here, but if you really expect me to stay and have dinner with you after the way you behaved when—'

'I've apologised for that,' he broke in. 'And I'd like to explain how it happened. Besides, I do have a legitimate reason for wanting to talk to you—a business reason.'

'Oh? What?'

'Let's talk about that over dinner, shall we?' His fingers loosed their hold on her arm and slid down to her hand, her left hand, which still bore traces of the bruises he had put there. Remaining very close to her, he lifted her hand, glanced at the bruises and back into her eyes. 'I hurt you,' he murmured. 'I'm sorry.' And he lifted her hand to press his lips there, sending sparks down her arm to jolt her heart.

Elizabeth hung there, breathless and troubled by the effect he had on her. Her throat seemed thick with an odd sort of panic whose cause she could not identify.

'Mr Delaval—' she began, and stopped when he gave her a smile of devastating charm.

Echoing his words on the beach, he said softly, 'My friends call me Mike.'

CHAPTER THREE

The orchids lay beside her place, vivid orange flecked with crimson and gold, echoing the colours of the sunset sky. Beyond huge windows as the sun went down lights pricked out in the village below, and the glow of floodlights brightened on the ancient castle crowning the opposite headland. Mike Delaval had organised a secluded table for two, hidden from other diners by a screen covered in climbing plants. Two slim red candles flickered between them.

Feeling as though this could not be happening, Elizabeth stared at the impressive menu. She finally chose a consommé that would be light on her stomach, and agreed to her escort's suggestion that she try the lobster dish, a speciality of the house, as a main course.

'What wine would you prefer?' he asked.

'No wine for me,' she said swiftly. 'I'm driving.'

'Perrier water, then?'

For the first time since coming into the restaurant, she made herself look at him, grateful that he hadn't insisted about the wine. Even one glass would, she knew, have gone straight to her head. 'Thank you.'

Calmly, in full control of the situation, he

gave their order to the waiter and glanced at Elizabeth. 'You look as though you're awaiting the executioner.'

'I'm still trying to make myself believe I'm here,' she replied. 'You . . . you aren't what I was expecting.'

'No? What did you expect?'

'I'm not sure. Someone older, I suppose. Someone more like Ben Sorensen. I thought *you* were a sailing instructor, or something.'

A faintly teasing light came into his eyes. 'Isn't that called leaping to conclusions?'

'I wasn't the only one, was I?' she said darkly.

One corner of his mouth turned down in what might have been regret. 'I'm afraid I didn't realise there were two young women connected with Belle Mer. I'd only heard of one. There was only one at Sorensen's funeral, so I heard. You?'

'Yes. Gayle said she was too upset to come. She lives in America, you know.'

'Yes, I did know, but I assumed she'd come over here to comfort her stepmother. As I said, I didn't realise there were two of you.'

'That still doesn't explain—' she began, and stopped as the waiter arrived with the first course.

For a while she concentrated on the consommé, a delicious cold jellied beef stock topped with tiny diced vegetables. Part of her seemed to be standing aside watching with

40

amazement as she sat in the company of Mike Delaval—a man she had hoped never to see again. What did he want of her?

He was eating some salad dish based on red cabbage and tiny slivers of veal, clearly having no problem with nerves. Her own stomach felt tight and the food seemed to be battling its way down. Perhaps, she thought, she ought to have had a glass of wine to relax her.

At last her dish was empty and she toyed with her water glass, watching candlelight flash rainbows in cut crystal. Unspoken questions and puzzles lay heavy on her mind as from her eye corner she watched the glint of a gold signet ring on Mike's little finger, matching the gleam of gold cufflinks just visible in the shadow of his sleeve. He had attractive hands, strong and long-fingered.

'You never met Gayle,' she said. 'You can't have done, or you wouldn't have mistaken me for her. She looks nothing like me.'

'No, I never met her,' he replied, his voice edged with harshness. 'By the time I came home she had done her worst and gone back to America, leaving a trail of disaster behind her—bruised egos, damaged feelings—not to mention broken marriages.'

Elizabeth lifted her eyes to his, seeing his mouth twist with disgust.

'She wasn't choosy,' he said. 'Married or single, it made no difference to her, so long as they were male, and breathing. Oh, I heard a great deal about Ben Sorensen's daughter, I assure you.'

'So you set out to teach her a lesson?'

Shrugging, he laid knife and fork across his plate. 'Arrogant of me, I agree. Perhaps I overreacted. But no, it wasn't premeditated. It was just that when you started for Belle Mer and I realised who you must be, I was so angry . . . I could have wrung your neck!'

'You made that very obvious,' Elizabeth said sharply. 'You frightened me to death! But if I *had* been Gayle, it would have been different. She'd have reacted differently—and so would you.'

A frown made a little V between his brows. 'How do you mean?'

'Gayle is sure of herself. She's beautiful, and she knows how to use her sex-appeal. Even you might not have remained immune. Oh . . . what's the point of arguing about it? I'm *not* Gayle. Another time, Mr Delaval, I suggest you get your facts straight before you start terrorising helpless women.'

He seemed to have stopped listening. His glance ran slowly over her shining hair, piled in errant curls with sun-gold wisps trailing on to the curve of her cheek. He examined every contour of her face, her mouth, her rounded chin, the graceful line of her throat rising from the low neckline of her dress.

Catching her breath, Elizabeth threw up a hand to fiddle with her necklet, instinctively

42

attempting to hide herself from his questing gaze. Her movement made his eyelids flicker, showing her the frank sensuality in slumbrous blue eyes. The man was outrageous!

'You think you're not beautiful?' he asked softly. 'On the contrary, Elizabeth.'

His deep voice spoke her name as though it were a caress. Soft colour flooded her cheeks, making her eyes extra bright. 'I wasn't asking for compliments.'

'I'm sure you weren't. You're not that sort of girl, are you?'

Realising she was in danger of losing track of her common sense, Elizabeth leaned back in her chair, mentally shaking herself before saying crisply, 'You don't know the first thing about me, Mr Delaval. And this is hardly the sort of conversation for a business dinner. Perhaps you'd be kind enough to tell me your real reason for bringing me here.'

'Later,' he replied, and sat back as the waiter brought the next course, lobster meat cooked in a rich creamy sauce and served in the shell accompanied by fluffy rice and salad.

Elizabeth stared at her portion, which looked enormous. This evening was not going at all as she expected. Mike Delaval was unpredictable, dangerously so. He had a knack of making her feel as if she were floundering in quicksand with imminent risk of drowning. Never before had she met a man so capable of reminding her that she was . . . she sought for the word. Vulnerable? Alone and defenceless? Less strong than he? All of that was true, but it didn't express everything. Basically, what he made her feel, she realised, was totally, wiltingly *female*. And it was not a feeling she liked; she preferred to be in control of herself.

'So tell me about yourself,' he suggested. 'You don't live permanently at Belle Mer, do you?'

'No. I've been living in London.'

'Doing what?'

'I'm a journalist.' Seeing the flare of surprise in his eyes, she added tartly, 'What did you think—that I sponged on my rich aunt? After she married Ben Sorensen, I stayed out of it. I had my job, and a flat I shared with two other girls. That's the way I prefer it. I like my independence.'

'Don't you have any parents?'

'A father, somewhere, though I haven't seen him for years. Aunt Helen brought me up. She's been like a mother to me. She gave up a great deal for my sake, so now it's my turn to take care of her.'

'How did she meet Sorensen?' he asked.

'She was here on holiday. I think they first met at the zoo.'

'Love at first sight,' he remarked with a derisive smile.

Elizabeth stiffened defensively, her eyes sparking. 'That has nothing to do with you, Mr Delaval!'

44

'You think not?' he asked with a lift of eyebrows. 'Well, perhaps you're right. How's the lobster?'

'Delicious, thank you.'

For a while they ate in silence, but despite the meal's wonderful taste and texture Elizabeth gave up her battle to clear her plate. As she laid down her knife and fork, her escort glanced questioningly at her.

'I thought you said it was delicious.'

'It is,' she sighed. 'I just don't seem to have much appetite lately. I might feel better if you'd tell me what it is you want to discuss. If it's about Belle Mer—'

She stopped as she sensed a sudden electricity in the air. Mike appeared turned to stone, only his eyes moving, searching hers in a way that made her scalp prickle with unease.

'What makes you think that?' he asked.

He *was* going to try to buy the house, Elizabeth thought. Oh, God! 'Someone suggested that it might be the reason behind this dinner invitation.'

'Someone? Who?'

'Nathan Frazer. He's the manager of—'

'I know who he is,' he cut in. 'I've never met him, but I know of him. Friend of yours, is he?'

'He's been a tower of strength, to both my aunt and me.'

'Looking after your best interests?'

It struck her that the conversation had taken an odd turn. 'Well . . . yes.'

'Is that why he phoned me to ask what I wanted to talk to you about?'

Wide-eyed with amazement, she stared at him. 'Nathan did?'

'Nathan did,' he agreed. 'Not that I told him anything. I rather gained the impression that he was afraid I might attempt to seduce you.'

Embarrassment robbed her of words. Heat rose in her face, but her eyes were held by blue ones as communicative as the sky. 'Really,' she managed with a breathless laugh, 'I can't think what made him do that. You must be mistaken.'

'So what did Mr Frazer think I might be after—apart from your body?'

Elizabeth swallowed the lump of disquiet in her throat, her instincts clamouring for escape. 'I'm sure he didn't mean . . . I'm sorry if he offended you. I had no idea he was going to phone you. I'm sure you're a perfect gentleman!'

He watched her enigmatically and the phrase 'perfect gentleman' hung between them, brittle with irony. His behaviour in the woods had proved that he was no gentleman, perfect or otherwise, and from the way he was looking at her now she knew that Nathan had had every reason to be concerned. Twin candleflames reflected in his eyes gave him the appearance of a demon. He was capable of almost anything.

With an impatient gesture, he broke that

mesmerising eye contact and returned his attention to his meal. 'We seem to have strayed from the point. What was Mr Frazer's opinion as to my motives?'

She drained her glass of Perrier water and took a deep breath. 'He said your family used to own Belle Mer, and you might want to buy it back.'

For a while he did not reply. He finished his lobster, sat back and touched a linen napkin to his lips, looking at her over it. 'Your Mr Frazer was wrong. Would you like dessert?'

'No, thank you,' she said at once. 'Just a coffee, please. But don't let me stop you.'

'I'm not too keen on sweet things,' he informed her. 'Bad for the teeth.' And he showed her his own strong white teeth in a smile that seemed menacing.

Whatever expression was on his face, Elizabeth realised, no warmth ever reached the depths of his eyes, which remained frozen, as though a part of him was shut away safe out of reach of any emotion. What was going on in the sharp mind behind those eyes?

A waiter brought coffee and Mike, having just said that he didn't like sweet things, liberally spooned brown sugar into his cup. Elizabeth watched him with perplexity, puzzling over him.

'If this isn't about Belle Mer . . .' she ventured.

'Elizabeth,' he chided, and unsettled every

nerve in her body by leaning to lay a warm hand on her wrist, 'do we have to discuss business right now? We've almost finished here. Let's go somewhere more private, shall we? I assume you brought your car?'

'Why—yes.'

'Then you can drive me home, and if you promise to behave I'll invite you in for a coffee.' His mouth twitched at this reversal of roles.

'If that's meant to be funny,' Elizabeth said stiffly, 'I'm afraid I don't appreciate the joke.'

'And anyway, you're sure I'm a perfect gentleman.'

She withdrew her hand, feeling it tingle where his fingers had rested. 'If you'll excuse me, I'll go and tidy myself up. I'll meet you out at the car—it's a white Granada.'

In the pink lights of the ladies' room, she let out a long breath, relaxing for the first time that evening. She repaired her make-up, pulling faces at herself in chagrin, wondering how much longer she could keep up the pretence of cool uninterest. Inside her, she felt like a mass of jelly, uncertain as a teenager on her first date. Mike Delaval did that to her, destroying her image of controlled sophistication. She must not, would not, let him see how deeply he affected her.

Why was she so nervous of him? Not because of who he was, surely? The fact was that, alone among the men she had met so far, he reached her where she was vulnerable—in the area of her being that longed to be swept up in strong arms and carried off by force. However unfashionable it might be to admit such feeble feminine desires, still she was sometimes weary of being tough and independent. She wished for someone warm and strong to lean on. But she had never met a man who seemed capable of fulfilling that need. Until now.

She straightened to regard her reflection critically, seeing how the shot-gold of her dress hugged her figure and swirled round her legs. Subconsciously she tried to see herself through Mike Delaval's eyes. Then drawing composure round her like a cloak, she went out into the car park, into cool night air with the sea sighing and the castle on its headland a mile away brightly lit by floodlamps.

Mike had not emerged from the restaurant yet. She climbed into the Granada and sat waiting, leaning across to unlock the passenger door as his tall figure appeared. He slid into the seat beside her, carrying the orchids she had forgotten.

'St Helier?' she enquired as she reversed out of the parking slot.

'Why do you assume I live in St Helier?' he asked.

'I thought . . . your hotel?'

'No, I just keep an office there. I have a place not far from Belle Mer, as a matter of

49

fact. Just head for home. I'll tell you when to turn off.'

The car slid down the twisting road, lights biting a bright tunnel through darkness beneath trees.

'Well!' Mike said after a while. 'This is pleasant. Usually I'm the one to drive my dates home. It's much nicer to sit here and watch you than look at the road.'

'Except that I'm not a date,' she reminded him.

'Aren't you?'

'Mr Delaval . . .'

'It's Mike,' he murmured, leaning closer, a long finger brushing against her cheek, making her flinch away.

'Please!' she exclaimed.

'Bothering you, am I?'

'I'm trying to drive! Unless you want us to end up in a hedge!'

'*That* bothered,' he murmured with dry mockery. 'I'm flattered.'

Thinking it best not to rise to the bait, Elizabeth gritted her teeth. Remaining calm was difficult with him so close, leaning towards her with his arm hooked round the back of her seat, his hand just brushing her shoulder. She was aware of his eyes on her profile and her nerves tied themselves in knots again. Striving for normality, she tried the gambit she had rehearsed as she waited for him.

'I seem to have been talking about myself all

50

evening. I don't know anything about you.'

'Why, what do you want to know?'

'Anything you'd care to tell me. I assumed you were French. With a name like Jean-Michel . . . You *are* Jean-Michel, I take it?'

'In Paris, yes. Here I'm Mike, as I keep telling you. My family originates in France, but my parents liked the Channel Islands so we mostly lived here. I'm bi-lingual, I'm thirty-four, I'm single, and I have all my own teeth. Anything else?'

'I should have known better than to ask,' Elizabeth said wryly. 'You seem determined not to tell me anything.'

'I'm surprised you're interested,' he replied.

She shot him an exasperated look, though the dim light in the car made his face unreadable. 'You write with hints about some mysterious business matter. You "suggest" we have dinner, so we can discuss it informally. And then I discover you're the same man who assaulted me in the woods. Naturally I'm curious. Wouldn't you be?'

'Yes,' he said thoughtfully. 'Yes, I would. Turn right at the next junction. Yes, here.'

The narrow lane wound between banked hedges where elms towered to a starlit sky. Within a mile or so, he directed her to take a left turn, then another right.

'What about you?' he asked eventually.

'What *about* me?' she countered.

'You and Nathan Frazer. Something going

on there?'

Elizabeth glanced at him guardedly. 'Why pick him out?'

'Just curious. He's not married, I gather. You did say he'd been a great help to you and your aunt. And he *did* phone me to warn me off.'

She turned her head to look at him with scorn. 'And two and two make five?'

Next second, he lunged for the wheel. 'Watch the road, you idiot!'

Quite what happened was never clear in Elizabeth's mind. They were at a bend. As she tried to correct the steering, the car slewed round. Tyres screamed, then the car stopped at an angle across the road. She felt giddy, her heart thumping. Beside her Mike swore loudly and bitterly, something about 'bloody women drivers'.

'Don't you dare criticise my driving!' she yelled back. 'I *was* watching the road. If you hadn't grabbed the wheel—'

'If I hadn't grabbed the wheel,' he said furiously, his eyes blazing at her in the faint light from the dashboard, 'we'd have gone into the bank.'

'I *knew* what I was *doing*!'

For a breathless moment hatred flared between them. Their faces were only inches apart. Then his glance dropped to her mouth and the mood changed subtly. All her nerve ends prickled and her skin broke into a delicate sweat as time stood still. She held her breath, her own eyes drawn to the firm mouth barely a whisper away. His scent seemed to drench her, a hint of aftershave mingled with his own musky aroma. Without any conscious volition from her, her lips plumped themselves in readiness to be kissed.

'You'd better switch the engine off,' he said. 'You've stalled it,' and he turned away, thrusting the door open to dive out of the car.

Elizabeth sat absolutely still for a moment, feeling as though she had been slapped and cursing herself for a fool. Stupidly, she felt rejected, though if he *had* kissed her she would have been livid. As always, he had managed to wreck her hard-held composure and reduce her to a quivering, receptive female, all with just one look.

Stiff with defiance, she restarted the car just as the door swung open and Mike ducked back inside.

'There's wet mud on the road,' he told her. 'Take it slowly.'

'Thank you for the advice,' she replied tartly, easing the car back into the correct position on the road.

After a while, he said, 'I'm sorry I yelled at you. If the truth be told, I make a lousy passenger. I feel much safer when I'm behind the wheel myself.'

'Then you shouldn't have asked me to bring you home,' she retorted. 'Why haven't you got transport of your own?'

'I have, but I took a taxi tonight. I knew you'd bring a car.'

So he had planned this, had he? Planned to get her back to wherever he lived, to get her alone. If he thought that corny ploy was going to work with Elizabeth Page then he was mistaken!

Soon, following his directions, she found herself heading between white gates on to a sweeping drive flanked by flowerbeds. At the top of a rise, lamps shed soft light across a white, Spanish-style bungalow. An archway in a wall led to an enclosed courtyard, where at Mike's instruction she parked the car. Tubs of flowers dotted the paving, and leaves twined round a fretwork trellis which roofed the courtyard.

'Now we'll have that coffee,' said Mike, leaving the car.

Since he still hadn't told her the purpose of this meeting, Elizabeth climbed out and looked around her. Beyond the trellis, stars beamed down from a velvet-blue sky, twinkling brightly, fascinating her so much that she almost walked into Mike. She drew back as if she had been stung and he gave her a humourless smile, showing her the orchids he was holding.

'You forgot these. You must let me pin them on for you.'

'It's a bit late for that,' she said, taking the

54

flowers. 'I'll put them in water when I get home.'

'Right. Well, come into the house. There's a friend of yours who'll be glad to see you.'

As he opened the door, she understood, for with a woof of pleasure Bran came rushing to leap round them both, quivering with pure delight.

'Idiot dog,' Mike said fondly, catching Bran's collar to push him outside. 'Go have a run, boy.' He closed the door, turning to look at Elizabeth through his lashes. 'Make yourself at home. I'll get the coffee.'

Following his gesture, she ventured through a reeded glass door set in an archway and found herself in a spacious sitting room. Another door at the far side must lead to the front hall. Rugs strewed polished wooden floors, with woven hangings on the walls. The upholstery was unbleached linen, chairs and settee strewn with bright-coloured cushions, and other furniture was made of clean-lined, shining wood. Two pairs of crossed swords flanked a fireplace large enough to roast an ox, and in one corner a big, paper-shaded lamp sent a warm yellow glow across the room.

Elizabeth perched on a large armchair, sitting erect on the edge of deep cushions, feeling ill at ease and not at all certain she had done the right thing in coming here. The orchids in her hand still glowed with sunset colours and she touched the petals with an appreciative finger. Bringing flowers had been a nice gesture—or was it the classic move of a seducer? Flowers, dinner by candlelight, and now coffee in his dim-lit home. The only things missing were soft music and, of course, the wine which might have mellowed her.

With a grimace of distaste, she laid the orchids on the low coffee table.

After a while, Mike reappeared with a laden tray which he set down beside the orchids and proceeded to pour coffee. Having handed her a cup, he lounged back on the broad settee. He had removed his jacket and tie, leaving his white shirt unbuttoned, the cuffs rolled back to display a gold watch on one brown wrist.

'How do you like the house?' he asked.

'It's very nice.'

'And how's your aunt?'

'Making slow progress. Please . . . can we stop making conversation? If you have something to say to me, I wish you'd say it.'

Frowning, Mike leaned with elbows on knees staring down into the coffee cup in his hands. 'Actually, I wasn't making idle conversation. Your aunt's health is relevant to what I have to say.'

'Oh?'

'Yes.' He slowly lifted his head to fix her with sombre eyes. 'Elizabeth . . . you may not believe this, but I'm finding it just as difficult as you are. Bear with me for a while, will you? I want to ask you a few questions—to get the whole picture straight. Do you mind?'

More and more puzzled, she shrugged. 'I suppose not.'

'To begin with—from things you've said tonight, I gather that your aunt intends to stay on at Belle Mer.'

'She does. Why shouldn't she? It's her home, even if Ben has left it to Gayle. Gayle more or less promised that she could stay, soon after the accident. And Ben probably made provision in the will for—'

'Ah, yes,' he interrupted heavily. 'The will.' He held up a hand to stop her protests. 'Okay, I know you're going to tell me it's none of my business, but I'm afraid it's all part of the same thing. Have you actually seen the will?'

'No, of course not. It's nothing to do with me. I'm not a beneficiary.'

'Has your aunt seen it?'

'No, I don't think so. She's been too ill. The solicitor's been handling everything. And I really can't see why—'

'I'm coming to that,' he said, reaching to set his cup on the table. 'What I'm trying to establish is that you're only making assumptions about Belle Mer. If you don't know what's in the will—'

'I don't care what's in the will! As long as it gives my aunt the right to live at Belle Mer, that's all that matters.'

His mouth compressed into a tight line, increasing the hard glitter in eyes turned black by the dim lighting. 'And suppose it doesn't?'

Controlling herself with an effort, Elizabeth placed her own cup on the table, though she was shaking so much she almost tipped it over. She got to her feet, her hands clenched. 'I don't know what you're trying to do, Mr Delaval. If you want to make an offer for the house, you should get in touch with Gayle, not me. But I doubt if she'll sell it. Not even she would turn her stepmother out on to the streets.'

He wrenched himself upright, glowering, said, 'Just wait here a minute,' and strode off via the far glass door to a shadowed hallway.

Elizabeth waited, trembling because she was terrified of what he was going to say.

He returned with a sheaf of legal-looking documents which he tossed on to the table and stood glaring at her over them. 'You want to read those?'

'Why, what are they?'

'They're the deeds to Belle Mer,' he informed her in a voice that fell on her ears like the tolling of a doom-laden bell. 'I had a feeling you wouldn't believe me, so I got them from my lawyers. Ben Sorensen didn't own that house, Elizabeth. It had stood empty for a while, so my grandfather was persuaded, after a lot of hassle, that it would do no harm to lease it out for a while. *That's* what Ben Sorensen did—he leased Belle Mer from my grandfather.'

Numb with shock, she lifted haunted eyes

from the documents to his grim dark face. 'Leased it? For how long?'

'The lease expires at the end of this month,' he said slowly and clearly as if to fix the fact in her stunned mind. 'I've delayed telling you because of your aunt's condition, but you had to know sooner or later. You see, when my grandfather died last year, he left the house to me. Belle Mer is *mine*, Elizabeth. And I want it back.'

CHAPTER FOUR

Elizabeth was calm now—much too calm, her reactions cushioned by shock. She sat in the chair, sipping a fresh cup of coffee, her face deathly pale but controlled, only her eyes revealing her inner panic. Having removed the tray, to set it on the floor, Mike seated himself on the sturdy low table in front of her, watching her with an expression that veered between exasperation and unwilling sympathy.

'I didn't mean for it to come out that way,' he said. 'But there was no easy way to tell you. I'm sorry about it, but your aunt will have to find somewhere else to live.'

'You don't understand,' Elizabeth breathed, a catch in her voice. 'She may not be able to afford anywhere else. And if Ben misled her . . . if she can't stay at Belle Mer . . . it will probably kill her.'

He stood up, running a hand through his hair as he moved away restlessly. 'Oh, come on! There's no need to be melodramatic about it.'

'I'm not being melodramatic,' she said, hearing the emptiness in her own voice. 'It's the simple truth. Knowing that she could stay at Belle Mer is all that's kept her going. Why did Ben lie to her? He let her believe he owned that house.'

'He *was* trying to buy it,' said Mike. 'Apparently he'd been bombarding my grandfather with offers, and he had started trying to negotiate an extension to the lease. Presumably he thought I'd relent if he offered me enough money. He didn't know he was going to die so soon. But he did die, Elizabeth. I'm sorry, but Belle Mer belongs to me and I want it.'

'Couldn't you . . . couldn't you let us rent it, maybe? We might be able to afford that, especially if I can get a job.'

'No,' he said, flatly and definitely. 'If I'd had any say in the matter, it wouldn't have been leased in the first place. I always planned to move back there. It's my home. My parents lived there. I grew up there. My father had the renovations done, and the swimming pool built. It has always been understood that one day the house would be mine and I'd make my home there.'

'But . . .' She glanced round at the lovely room she was sitting in, 'you've got this place. You don't need Belle Mer. It's huge for a man on his own.'

'That's my business. I want your aunt out, because I want to move in. It's as simple as that.'

Elizabeth was trembling, the cup almost rattling in her hand. Bending, she slipped the cup on to the tray and sat with her hands clenched in her lap, her eyes on one of the bright hangings. 'It's not simple at all. My aunt is very ill. If she gets wind of this . . .' Lifting her head, she looked at him with tears glazing her eyes. 'They've warned me time and time again—no upsets. A quiet life from now on. She loved Ben Sorensen. She trusted him. She never asked for much. All she wants is to go home to Belle Mer where her happy memories are. That's the only thing that's brought her through.'

'Well, I'm sorry. You'll just have to find some way to break the news gently. As for money . . . get her lawyers to fight for it.'

Elizabeth stood up, shaking visibly. 'You haven't been listening! A court case would be just as bad—Gayle would fight it all the way. Oh, you don't care about anything, do you? It would just suit you if my aunt died and got out of your way. You're inhuman, Mike!'

'Listen to me,' he ordered, hard hands fastened on her shoulders, his face darkened by anger. 'I've put off telling you until now because I knew your aunt wasn't strong. I didn't want to worry her. I'm not going to throw you out at the end of the month, if that's what you're afraid of. You can stay at Belle Mer until you find somewhere else. I won't even charge you rent. You can be my guests.'

This crumb of kindness, small though it seemed at the time, made tears press harder against the dam of her self-control. She felt alone and afraid. For the first time in her adult life, she simply didn't know how to handle this dilemma.

'I can't tell her,' she whispered brokenly. 'It will kill her. Oh, Mike!'

The dam burst and, unable to stop herself, she leaned on him weeping helplessly, needing comfort and support. She felt him stiffen, his hands braced as if to push her away, then his arms slid round her. Her tears soaked into his white dress shirt, but she only knew that he was warm and strong and she needed his strength to protect her.

He laid his cheek on her hair, cradling her as if she were a child while sobs racked through her. Her thoughts went crazy with fear. She kept seeing her aunt's face, as it would look when Helen discovered she had been cruelly misled by the husband she had adored. Bereft, emptied of hope, Helen would give up trying. Elizabeth could foresee it as surely as if she were psychic.

She clung to Mike in desperation, her arms tightly round his strong body, her fingers digging into his broad back in her agony of distress. Very slowly, he bent his head until his lips touched her cheek, moving gently in whisperlight kisses. Hardly knowing what she was doing, she turned her face and let her mouth meet his.

His lips caressed hers softly, comforting and coaxing, so that warmth flooded up through her entire body and seemed to explode in her brain. She surged up to wrap her arms round his neck and fasten her mouth on his, trying to lose herself in a whirlpool of sensation that momentarily blotted out her frightened thoughts.

He held her closer and closer, his arms threatening to crush her as his mouth possessed hers in a fever of hunger. Elizabeth locked her fingers in his hair, holding him down to her, returning passion for passion. Wildfire built inside her, so that her body adjusted itself to fit the contours of his, feeling the heat of him, and the unmistakable desire.

Faintly, as if from a million miles away, she heard Bran barking, and her sanity returned with a jolt. What was she doing? Mike's hands ran over her back, exploring the shape of her, urging her ever more tightly against him. With a wordless cry, she wrenched her mouth free and he bent his head to bury his face in her throat, his lips burning her skin.

'Bran's barking,' she whispered dazedly.

'Let him bark,' he muttered.

'No! Mike!' Laying her hands to his shoulders, she forced his upper body away from her, seeing his face blank, his eyes glazed with desire. Suddenly the contact of their bodies shocked her and she tore free of him, crying, 'What are we doing?'

'You know what we're doing,' he said raggedly, reaching for her again.

Elizabeth evaded him, stepping backwards and sideways. Her heel caught in the rug and she sprawled across the settee with her skirt flying above her knees. Seeing his glance drawn to her legs, she reached to jerk the skirt down. 'Mike, please! Bran wants to come in.'

For a second or two he stared down at her, anger and frustration warring in his face; then he swung on his heel and went to let the dog in.

Horrified by her own behaviour, Elizabeth laid a cool hand to her burning face as she stood up, glancing around for her handbag. What had possessed her? What must Mike think of her now? She had never behaved like that before. Never.

As she smoothed down her dress, Bran's claws pattered on the polished floor and the dog's big, sinuous shape shouldered past the glass door. He came quietly towards her, tail wagging, ears pricked, eyes bright, and allowed her to stroke his great head. Thank God for

Bran, she thought fervently. If it hadn't been for him, she and Mike might have made violent love right here in this room, and completed the disaster of this terrible evening.

She was aware of Mike standing by the open door to the rear hall, but she couldn't look at him. She concentrated on the dog, stroking his head and his floppy ear.

'Well?' Mike said eventually.

'You'll have to give me time to think of something,' she replied, her voice an unsteady croak. 'I don't know what I'm going to do, but if there's a way I'll find it.'

'And if not?'

She looked up, hardly seeing him for the mist across her eyes. 'There has to be a way. There *has* to be!'

On impulse, she picked up the orchids as she began to walk towards him. He stepped aside in silence, allowing her into the narrow hall, where she turned, her eyes on the flowers. 'Thank you for these. And for dinner. And for coffee.'

'Brought up to be polite, were you?' he asked with cool scorn.

Her eyes stung and she turned away, not wanting him to see how easily he could upset her. She was not herself that night. Nothing was normal. As she left the house, Mike said, 'I'll be in touch,' and then he closed the door. She was alone in the starlit courtyard, clematis leaves stirring above her in the night breeze, and her only companions her wretched thoughts.

*   *   *

She hardly slept that night. Tossing and turning in her bed at Belle Mer, she went over and over the problem, finding no solution. And in the midst of her worried thoughts she kept returning to the memory of Mike Delaval's arms around her. Illogically, she wished he was with her now, to hold her and stop the torment of thoughts that plagued her. But he had not been the one to reach for her: *she* had reached for *him.* She had accepted his comfort, sought his kisses, and then been horrified when he reacted as any normal male would have done. The shame was hers, all hers, and she doubted if she could ever face Mike Delaval again.

In the morning, having decided that the first thing to do was to make sure of her facts, she telephoned her aunt's solicitor at his home. Even though it was a Saturday, Mr Lenton agreed to see her and invited her to come over to his home in St Helier.

She discovered him in the garden, mowing the lawn, his usual business suit discarded for a pair of flannels and a flowered shirt, with a floppy hat protecting his bald head from the sun. He invited her to sit down on his rustic bench, and his wife brought a tray of cold drinks.

For a while they chatted about her aunt, the weather, his garden. Elizabeth recalled his coming to visit her in the first awful days when she had not known whether her aunt would live or die. He had wanted to talk about the will then, though he had warned her it was a complicated business and she had told him to do whatever he thought best. At the time, she had been unable to think of anything but her aunt.

'The papers are at my office, of course,' he said now, regarding her in a troubled fashion. 'But I can remember the gist. What is it you want to know?'

'Is my aunt one of the beneficiaries?' she asked.

'Yes, of course. The bulk of the estate goes to his daughter, as you know. Shares, property, capital investments . . . But for your aunt there's the income from some shares, and a few personal things.'

'When you say she has the income, that means she can't sell the shares, doesn't it?'

'Yes, I'm afraid so. The income is hers during her lifetime, but on her death the shares revert to Mr Sorensen's daughter. I'm sure your aunt knows that.'

Sighing, Elizabeth glanced round the garden. Its blaze of spring colour looked garish at that moment. 'She does, and she accepts it—she's not the mercenary sort. Mr Lenton . . . you haven't said anything about Belle Mer

67

itself. Is that part of Ben's estate, too?'

'Oh, no, my dear,' he said at once. 'I thought you knew. We were trying to extend the lease, but the owner wasn't keen on the idea. Mr Sorensen died before anything could be agreed. But there's no need to worry. I've been in touch with the owner and, in the circumstances, he's in no hurry to repossess. You'll have ample time to make other arrangements for your aunt. Her income will cover a small mortgage, I'm sure.'

'Jean-Michel Delaval,' Elizabeth murmured, half to herself.

Mr Lenton looked surprised. 'You know him?'

'I've met him. That's why I'm here. I'd hoped you'd tell me it was a mistake, but . . .' Her head felt heavy with unshed tears as she stood up. 'Never mind. Thank you, Mr Lenton.'

'If there's any way I can help . . .' he said anxiously.

'Thank you, but no one can help. It will take a miracle.'

*   *   *

She returned to Belle Mer, oppressed by the heat of the day. Finch told her that Nathan had called. Elizabeth knew that Nathan would be anxious to know what had happened between her and Mike Delaval, but she

68

couldn't possibly tell him the truth.

She would phone him later, when she had decided what to say to her aunt. How could Ben have done this to his wife? Being Ben, he wouldn't have liked to confess that he had been baulked by Jean-Michel Delaval's stubbornness. He could not possibly have foreseen that Helen would learn the truth when she was so ill, without him to support her.

Perhaps Elizabeth could delay telling her aunt anything until she was stronger. Perhaps she could persuade Helen that Belle Mer was not so important—except that she knew she could do no such thing. To Helen, Belle Mer was more than just a house: it was the home where she had been all too briefly happy with a man she had adored.

Ben should never have let Helen get so fond of the place without telling her the truth! And if Mike hadn't been so immovable none of this need have happened. Why was he so anxious to have this house? He could have any house he chose, anywhere in the world. He was a single man, and Belle Mer was meant for a family.

Perhaps—her flying thoughts congealed with dismay at the idea—perhaps he was planning to get married and raise his own family here!

Sick of the endless sorry-go-round in her mind, she ran up to her room, tossed off her clothes and put on a black bikini with a towelling robe. She needed exercise, and where better than the swimming pool?

She slipped through the house and came into the annexe where the pool lay shimmering blue, with a bright shaft of sunlight lying across it. All down the wall facing the garden, big glass doors stood open to the air, with a patio beyond.

Throwing her wrap across a wicker chair in a shadowed corner, Elizabeth dived into the pool and began an energetic crawl up and down the blue length, trying to lose herself in physical action. At the deep end there was shadow, while the shallow end lay in blinding sunlight. She swam on, regulating her strokes and mentally ticking off the lengths, trying to go to the limit of her strength. At eleven lengths her arms were aching, but she pushed on and completed twelve and turned, exhausted, thinking that thirteen lengths might be unlucky. Superstition, silly though it was, made her turn for the side of the pool.

She hung on the side for a while, catching her breath and letting her heartbeat return to normal, with her face lifted to the sun. Light beat against her closed eyelids; visible as a pink glow. Eventually she hauled herself out, dripping, pushing her heavy hair back over her shoulder as she made for the shaded corner where she had left her robe.

The sunlight must be playing tricks on her

eyes—it looked as though someone was sitting in that chair.

Coming into the shade, Elizabeth stopped, blinking hard as the figure in the chair rose and said evenly, 'Good morning. Lovely day.'

'Mike?' she said blankly. 'What are you doing here?'

'You're not very original,' he commented. 'That's exactly what you said last night. I did tell you I'd be in touch.'

Now that she could see properly again, she was made vividly aware of her half-naked, dripping state. His blue eyes were taking advantage of the sight of almost every inch of her.

He was holding her wrap, she realised. She held out a hand for it. 'Please.'

'This?' He glanced at the wrap as if wondering whether to withhold it, then with a slight smile handed it over and watched her pull it on. 'Spoilsport,' he chided. 'What's the matter—afraid I might lose control of myself again? That was a very tempting invitation you offered last night.'

Her cheeks burned dully as she knotted the belt of her robe. 'I was upset—I didn't know what I was doing. Why are you here? You said you'd give me time.'

'So I will. How long will it take for you to find somewhere else for your aunt to live?'

'I—' Suddenly she was choked again with tears. A hand to her eyes, she turned away

71

from him, taking a deep breath to control herself. 'I don't know. I went to see the solicitor this morning, and he confirmed everything you said.'

'Why, did you think I was lying?'

'No. No, but I hoped, somehow, that it was all a mistake. Mike . . .' Turning, she threw out a hand in appeal, 'I can't do anything yet—I just can't! If you saw her lying there, looking so fragile and trying so hard to be brave . . . Losing Ben is bad enough. If she knows she's losing Belle Mer, too, it might be too much for her to take. I can't do that to her. Not now. Not yet.'

'I know,' he said gravely. 'I called in at the nursing home earlier and talked to her doctor. I told him I was a close friend of yours, and anxious to know the truth about your aunt's condition. He didn't go into details, but he told me enough. To be honest, I thought you were exaggerating last night.'

'But I wasn't.'

'No, obviously not.'

He watched her with sombre, veiled eyes and she stared back sadly. Impasse, she thought. They could delay breaking the news for a short while, but it wouldn't change anything.

Mike seemed taller than ever when she stood in bare feet. He had his fists in the pockets of blue jeans and he wore a form-fitting shirt with a laced opening unfastened to

72

show a wedge of tanned chest dusted with dark hairs. His face was still, tousled hair falling over his forehead almost into shadowed eyes, and his mouth was set in carved lines.

A quiver ran through her as she remembered the heat of that mouth, and the firm muscles that had made her flesh seem to melt. Her senses would never forget how he had felt, and how he had made her feel.

Troubled by the trend of her thoughts, she said, 'So what are we going to do?'

'I wish I knew,' Mike replied with a grimace. 'I don't fancy having your aunt on my conscience, but . . . Hell!' He threw himself down in the chair, making the wicker creak. 'Why did my grandfather have to lease the place to Sorensen at all? He *knew* I'd be coming back here.'

'But no one knew the complications that would arise,' she reasoned. 'I . . . I don't suppose you'd consider waiting for a while? My aunt's not an old woman. She might, in time, recover more fully than anyone expects.'

'How much time, for instance? Months? Years? No, I'm not prepared to wait. Couldn't you persuade her that the place is too big for her on her own?'

'I've already said something of the kind, but she won't listen. She just doesn't want any more upheavals. Besides, she won't be on her own. I'll be here, too.'

He glanced at her from under frowning

brows. 'And what happens when you want to get married?'

The question made her mind go blank. She hadn't thought of that. 'I shan't.'

'What, never?' he asked in disbelief. 'Isn't there some chap in London chewing his nails because you're over here without him?'

'No, there isn't.'

He came out of the chair in one lithe movement that reminded her how powerful he was. Powerful, male, totally alive and pulsatingly attractive. 'Then what about Nathan Frazer?'

'Oh, for goodness' sake!' she exclaimed. 'You asked me that last night. I told you—'

'You didn't tell me anything at all,' he argued, making a move towards her. 'We were interrupted, if you remember.'

She did remember, all too clearly, those breathless moments in the car after it skidded on mud. Chill fingers ran up her spine, bringing her out in goose-pimples. 'There's nothing to tell. Honestly.'

'Isn't there?' he demanded, and gestured impatiently. 'Then why, when he phoned me, did he sound so possessive over you?'

'I've no idea,' Elizabeth muttered through a constricted throat. 'It's not because of any encouragement he's had from me. I didn't know he would phone you. He had no right to—what I do is none of his concern.'

She found herself edging backwards, afraid

of the black frown on his face. She held out a hand as if to prevent his advance, saying nervously. 'Anyway—Mike—what about you? Why are you so impatient to have Belle Mer? So you can get married?'

'Watch it!' he roared. The same instant, Elizabeth found herself over the edge of the pool, arms flailing as she tried to regain her balance. Then Mike was beside her, scooping her away from danger, his arms closing round her like steel bands.

'Phew! Thanks!' She pressed her hands on his upper arms, expecting him to let her go, but instead his hold tightened.

'That,' he said, watching her mouth with an intimate hunger that made her sweat, 'is not a bad idea.'

'What isn't?'

'Marriage.' A big hand at the base of her spine forced her hips into close contact with his and her eyes widened as she realised how aroused he was.

Licking suddenly-dry lips, she stared at him tensely. 'Marriage to whom?'

'You know to whom,' he growled in a fierce undertone, moving his body suggestively against hers. The pupils of his eyes had widened, almost eclipsing the blue. Despite herself, she felt her body begin to respond with flickers of desire starting deep inside her.

Her lips prickled as his gaze fixed on the reddened curves of her mouth, but when he

75

dropped his head she turned away. His lips grazed her jaw and fastened on the tendon in her neck, moving down to her collarbone under the lapel of her robe.

Elizabeth closed her eyes, willing herself to remain stiff and defiant in his arms. 'There's more to marriage than that,' she breathed.

'Yes,' he said against her skin, and lifted his head, his fingers forcing her chin up so that her eyes met his cynical, burning gaze. 'There's a home here at Belle Mer for your aunt, with me paying all the bills, for as long as she needs it.'

As she drew breath to reply, he kissed her full on her parted lips, holding her face up to his. His mouth moved sensually, ravaging and invading her senses. She strained to get away, her fingers clawing at his shirt while her whole body came totally alive. He felt hard and demanding against her. The warm male scent of him assailed her with every breath, overwhelming her resistance.

She lifted her hands intending to strike him, pull his hair, tear at his ears, but instead, her fingers caught in the waves of his hair and stroked the live column of his neck. With a shudder, she relaxed against him, giving herself up to the tide of desire flooding through her.

His hand left her jaw and spread across her throat as he bent over her. Confidently, he reached inside her wrap and cupped the sweet

76

weight of her breast, barely covered by the bikini.

'No!' She brought her elbow down sharply, knocking that cavalier hand away. Caught by surprise, he released her.

Elizabeth brought up her hand and slapped his face with all the strength she possessed. The blow jarred her arm and left her hand tingling painfully as she hung there horrified, watching his face darken with anger. On his cheek, the white mark of her hand turned dull red, and every muscle in his powerful frame was clenched.

'On the other hand,' he snarled, 'I could just throw you out at the end of the month and let you do what you damn well please!'

'You wouldn't,' she choked. 'Oh, please . . . I'm sorry I hit you; but you shouldn't touch me like that. I hardly know you!'

He seemed to relax, his anger giving way to grim mockery. 'Oh, you know me well enough, Elizabeth. Your flesh and your blood know me, as mine know you. We're fated, can't you feel it?'

A swift step brought him close to her again. She tensed as his hands came softly on her waist and he studied her upturned face. 'I want you,' he told her. 'I think I've wanted you from that very first day. That's what made me extra angry when I thought you were Gayle Sorensen—I thought I was in danger of succumbing to your charms like every other man on the island. But you're not the woman I thought. You're fresh, beautiful . . . And you want me, too.'

As she began to deny this, a cold smile touched his mouth. He shook his head, pulling her closer to him. 'Oh, yes, you do. You can't deny what you tell me without words. So why don't we make it legal? You need Belle Mer for your aunt, and if you become my wife I'll let her live here with us. Fair exchange, Elizabeth.'

She shuddered convulsively, trying to shut out the voice inside her that urged her to accept this monstrous proposal. 'But I don't love you.'

'What difference does that make?'

'A lot of difference!' Her voice was unsteady and she kept her hands braced against his chest to keep him that little distance away. 'I'd never marry anyone unless—'

'Don't be naïve!' he broke in. 'You know what love is? It's just a temporary insanity that never lasts. If you're not careful, you can make a damn fool of yourself over it.'

She was shaking so much she could hardly think, except about what his proximity was doing to her, but she recognised the underlying bitterness behind his words. 'Is that what happened to you? You made a fool of yourself over some woman?'

'Or she made a fool of me,' he replied, 'which is probably nearer the truth. I've been down that road, and I didn't like the view. I'll never let another woman get such a hold on me. But you can have anything else you want. I'm not a poor man. You'd be amply rewarded for your wifely favours. And at least we'd both know exactly where we stand.'

She couldn't do it, she thought. Not even for her aunt's sake. 'It's out of the question. It would be a sham.'

'Who's to know that, except you and me?' Mike gave her a smile that was just a curving of his mouth, leaving his eyes curiously lifeless. Releasing her, he stepped away to stretch himself in the sunlight like a lazy panther. 'But the choice is yours. Are you going to see your aunt this afternoon?'

The thought of having to face Helen and tell bright lies about her 'dinner date' made Elizabeth's head pound with despair. 'Yes, but I won't tell her anything.'

'You won't need to,' he said meaningfully. 'Your face will be enough. You're not very good at prevaricating, Elizabeth. If she knows you at all, she'll guess something is wrong, and if you don't tell her she'll worry all the more.'

It was true, she thought wretchedly. Helen, above all people, knew her too well to be fooled for long.

'Why don't you invite me to stay for lunch?' Mike suggested. 'Let's talk about this calmly. You'll see that I'm right.'

CHAPTER FIVE

At his suggestion, Elizabeth showed her unnerving visitor over the house, where he examined the changes Ben and Helen had made in décor and furnishing. Most of them met with his approval. One bedroom had been his own when he was young, he told Elizabeth. It was the room *she* was now using. She moved swiftly on, into the master suite.

'Slept separately, did they?' asked Mike with raised eyebrows as he surveyed the two beds in the big room.

'They were more comfortable that way,' Elizabeth said defensively. 'Ben suffered from insomnia.'

He glanced at her with a gleam in his eyes. 'We'll have to change that.'

Unable to reply, she retreated from the master suite.

At the end of the hall lay a small sitting room with its own balcony looking out over the garden and the woods. With its own bathroom, two adjoining bedrooms and a kitchenette, it had been intended as the nursery suite when the house was originally built.

'My aunt loves this room,' Elizabeth said, looking at the glass shelves filled with tiny ornaments which Helen collected.

'Seems ideal,' agreed Mike. 'She'll need a

lot of care, even when she's home, I assume. She can have this suite. We'll hire a nurse to look after her while she's convalescing.'

'There won't be any need for that! I can look after her.'

'You'll have enough to do, just being my wife,' he argued.

She bit her lip. 'I haven't said—'

'No, but you will. It's the most logical solution.'

In the back of her mind the voice of protest continued to be heard, though it grew fainter and fainter. Elizabeth began to wonder if she were a fool to quibble over an insubstantial thing like love. What mattered most was Helen's health and happiness.

If Helen had to be told that she must leave Belle Mer, it would be a bitter blow to a woman already enduring enough. Her income, and Elizabeth's, if she were able to find a job, might just cover a mortgage, but probably not for a house on Jersey. Helen would have to sell her furniture, and probably her jewellery, the few things Ben had given her during their brief marriage. It would be like wiping out those happy years. And Helen was bound to feel herself a burden on Elizabeth. The prospect was intolerable.

Over lunch, Mike talked of the ploys they might use to keep Helen in ignorance of their pact. He made it all sound logical, as though it were some business deal they were discussing.

His quick brain soon came up with answers to any problem Elizabeth envisaged—on a practical level, at least. Not once did he allude to the emotional aspect of the deal.

'We can tell her I'm buying the house from Gayle,' he decided. 'You don't have much contact with Sorensen's daughter, I gather.'

'She phoned once, after the accident,' Elizabeth replied. 'As far as I can tell, she doesn't give a damn what happens to my aunt from now on. But she might be surprised when she finds she hasn't been left Belle Mer.'

'Well, if she gets in touch, refer her to me. I'll soon settle that lady's hash for her.'

He would have what he wanted, and her aunt could stay, with an easy mind, in the home she loved. *And what about me?* Elizabeth wanted to cry. Oh, she would have everything she could want, anything money could buy, plus the relief of letting her aunt live without any more stress. She would also have a husband who was cold as ice, except at times when his blood ran hot.

As they talked, she watched him with a detached part of her mind, admiring his strong, classic features and the way his hair grew thick and springy. He spoke persuasively of how life would be when they were married—it had become 'when' rather than 'if' almost without Elizabeth's noticing.

'So what do you say?' Mike asked eventually. 'Shall we do it?'

She was glad he had phrased it so unromantically. If he had said 'Will you marry me?' it would have been just too farcical. 'I don't seem to have much choice,' she said.

'I'll be good to you,' he promised. 'I can be quite bearable when I'm not being crossed. You play your part and I'll play mine. Is it a deal?'

Why, she wondered, did she still long for something more? Marriage was the obvious answer to her problem. Her mind knew it, but deep inside her she wished it could have been different.

'You'll be wanting to shake hands on it next,' she said with an attempt at lightness which failed to remove the shadows from her eyes.

Smiling in that way he had, always with something held back, Mike came slowly out of his chair and walked round the table. 'I think a kiss would be more appropriate, don't you?'

Elizabeth stiffened. 'In the circumstances, no. I don't want you to kiss me, thank you.'

'Don't you?' He stood behind her chair, his hands rubbing her shoulders, his thumbs stroking her neck. When she tried to shake him off he bent with an arm across her throat, his mouth near her ear. 'You're such a liar, Elizabeth. How long do you think you can resist?'

'As long as it takes!' she hissed, trying to drag his arm away so that she could move. His

83

tongue licked round her ear very softly; and then he pressed his lips to the side of her throat. 'Don't do that!' she cried.

She breathed easily again as he moved away, his eyes glinting with grim humour. 'Shall we make it a month from now? I think I can wait a month before I move into Belle Mer, I mean. Okay?'

'Yes, fine,' Elizabeth croaked, more relieved than she dared admit even to herself. Thank God he hadn't insisted on a special licence and a rushed wedding. Thank God she would have a month's grace in which to prepare herself. In a month, anything could happen. Perhaps that longed-for miracle would occur and save her.

*   *   *

Mike drove her to the nursing home in his glossy pagoda-top Mercedes, which drew admiring glances as he pulled up by the entrance to let her out.

'I'll pick you up in about an hour,' he promised before driving away, leaving Elizabeth to face one of the most difficult hours of her life.

But, to her relief, her aunt already had a visitor—one of her friends, a woman named Hermione Bessamer, wife of a merchant banker. Mrs Bessamer monopolised the conversation, with Elizabeth adding a comment occasionally. The gossip seemed to entertain Helen, who looked brighter than she had done since the accident. But she kept throwing questioning looks at Elizabeth.

Eventually Mrs Bessamer took her leave, promising to come back again in a couple of days. As she departed, Helen smiled at Elizabeth, holding out a hand.

'Come closer. Goodness, Hermione does talk! It was kind of her to come, but I'm dying to hear about your date. Last night poor Nathan seemed quite out of sorts because of it. So, how did it go?'

'I had a wonderful time,' Elizabeth replied with what she hoped was the right amount of enthusiasm. 'The Cliff is a lovely place. Such views over St Fleur bay. And the food . . .'

'Never mind about the food,' Helen quipped, 'what about the feller? Oh, do tell me about him, love. How long have you known him?'

'A few weeks.' Few meaning two, near enough. 'I first met him on the beach in the cove. He has a Great Dane called Bran— terrified me at first, but he's friendly when you get to know him.'

Helen pursed her lips. 'Are you talking about your young man or his dog? You're being evasive, Elizabeth. He's not married, is he?'

'No, of course he's not! Good heavens . . . he's . . . good-looking, charming. About six foot two, dark-haired, athletic . . .'

'Does this paragon have a name?'

'Mike. Mike Delaval.'

Helen's brow furrowed. 'Delaval? Where have I heard that name before?'

'You can hardly miss it. His family has a lot of business connections in the islands. He's in charge of their operations here. Very high-powered. Actually, he's Jean-Michel—French ancestry.'

'And what else?' Helen asked quietly. 'There's something, I can tell.'

'There's nothing! Except . . . well, Ben locked horns with the Delavals a few times, I gather. I wasn't sure whether it would make any difference. It wasn't Mike's fault. He's been abroad until recently. You'll like him, Aunt Helen. I know you will.' Elizabeth had redoubled her efforts, forcing herself to sound a little shy, a little intense. Oddly enough, it wasn't difficult.

The doubts left Helen's face and she smiled. 'Do *you* like him? That's more to the point.'

'Yes, I do, very much. It's funny, you were only saying a couple of weeks ago that I ought to find someone, and now . . . I'd like you to meet him, and he wants to meet you. May I bring him in to see you tomorrow?'

'It sounds serious,' her aunt commented fondly.

'It is,' said Elizabeth. 'Very serious.'

The nurse came in to say that she thought

Helen had had enough excitement for one afternoon. Elizabeth kissed her aunt and slipped away, pausing in the corridor to take a deep breath and congratulate herself on negotiating the first hurdle. It would be easier from now on.

Glancing at her watch, she hurried out of the nursing home. She found herself watching for Mike's car with curiously mixed feelings. And then, with dismay, she saw Nathan Frazer's lean, bespectacled figure striding towards her.

'I hoped I'd catch you,' he said. 'I've phoned the house twice this morning. The first time you were out and the second time Finch said you had a guest for lunch, so I told him not to bother you. I've been going quietly mad wondering what happened last night.'

'It's nice of you to be concerned,' Elizabeth said, half her mind still watching for a blue Mercedes and hoping it wouldn't appear yet.

'Well, you were worried about it,' said Nathan. 'What did he want?'

'Only to have dinner with me.' She gave him her full attention, sorry that she had ever brought him into the situation. 'As a matter of fact, Nathan, I'd met him a couple of times before, though I only knew him as Mike. Getting me to have dinner that way was . . . his idea of a joke, you might say. Keeping me guessing. You know.'

He looked at her as if she had gone mad.

87

'No, I don't know. So he's a friend of yours—is that what you're saying? There wasn't any business matter?'

'It was entirely personal, I'm afraid,' she said, forcing a little laugh. 'I'm sorry you were worried, Nathan. I had a lovely evening.'

'With Jean-Michel Delaval,' he said flatly. 'Well, I just hope you know what you're doing. Are you aware he's a notorious ladykiller? A man like that—wealthy, charismatic, single— he collects women.'

Elizabeth flinched away. 'That's vicious gossip!'

'How can you be sure? I suppose you've fallen for him just like the rest. I really thought you had more sense.'

'Oh, did you?' She was angry now. 'Perhaps I have enough sense to judge from my own knowledge rather than listening to idle rumours. Why didn't you say anything the other day, when I asked you about him?'

'Because I thought it was just a business matter. And since then I've been asking around. I didn't realise he was so young, or that he was unattached.'

'Is that why you phoned him?' she demanded. 'Yes, he told me about that. I suppose you thought you were protecting me, but I'm quite capable of looking after myself, you know.'

Nathan blinked unhappily behind his glasses. 'That's what *I* thought, until I got mixed up with Gayle Sorensen. I just don't want you getting hurt, that's all. Gayle and Delaval are two of a kind. We're not in the same league, you and I. Elizabeth, don't let him—' He broke off, glancing behind her.

Before she could move, a hand fell on her shoulder, insinuating itself under her hair to rub the nape of her neck in a possessive way. Only one man would have the nerve to touch her like that.

'Hello, darling,' Mike said softly as he leaned to brush his lips across her cheek. 'Aren't you going to introduce me to your friend?'

She did so, with a simple, 'Nathan Frazer— Mike Delaval,' and watched as the two shook hands. Mike was smiling, friendly, apparently at ease, while Nathan seemed turned to stone.

'I've heard a lot about you, Mr Frazer,' said Mike. 'I gather you've been keeping an eye on Elizabeth and her aunt. I'm grateful, but from now on you can leave all that to me.'

'I trust Elizabeth won't cut herself off completely from her old friends,' Nathan said stiffly, adding to Elizabeth, 'You know where I'll be if you need me. 'Bye for now.'

As he strode rather jerkily away, Mike laid an arm round her shoulders. She had been appropriated: he was taking her over, and there was nothing she could do about it.

*   *   *

Her aunt adored him, naturally enough. At his charming best, Mike could be irresistible and at times even Elizabeth found herself forgetting that cold part of him which was shut away out of her reach. He made Helen laugh. He filled her sickroom with flowers, plied her with chocolates and brought her books and magazines. Within days, he had established himself as an integral part of their lives.

During the week, he arrived unexpectedly at Belle Mer and insisted on driving Elizabeth to the shopping precinct in St Helier, where he took her to the best jeweller's shop to buy an engagement ring.

'Any ring you'd like,' he said with an expansive gesture around the glittering trays.

Elizabeth, half dazzled, saw the assistant's eyes gleam as he scented profit. She gazed at the selection—diamonds, emeralds, rubies, sapphires; solitaires and clusters. Something in her rebelled. Mike might be able to force her into marriage, but he must not be allowed to think she could be bought.

Her eye fell on an attractive moderately-priced ring with three small diamonds grouped in a platinum setting like a round-cornered triangle. 'This one,' she said, picking it out.

She heard Mike catch his breath in disbelief. 'That one? Why?'

'Because I like it—it's pretty, and it won't be heavy to wear.'

He argued, and the assistant helped him, but she remained adamant and eventually Mike gave in, saying wryly, 'Well, at least I know I'm getting a thrifty woman!'

Wearing the ring, Elizabeth left the shop with Mike a pace behind her. Out in the pedestrian precinct, he took her arm and hustled her away, his face grim.

'I suppose you know you made me look like an idiot in there? You could have had any ring you chose.'

'And I chose this one,' she pointed out. 'It suits me fine. I'm really not interested in what your money can buy me, Mike.'

'You're a woman, aren't you? All women like expensive things.'

She turned her sea-green eyes on him. 'It depends what sort of woman you're talking about. For me, it's not the expense that matters, it's the reason for the gift.'

Ironically enough, though, when she later examined the ring more closely, she discovered that the triangle setting was in fact a heart. How romantic! Especially when it was the only heart involved in this charade.

When Helen saw the ring, and learned that there was to be a wedding very soon, she could not have been happier. Tearfully, she looked from Elizabeth's face to Mike's. 'I'm so glad for you both. And I love the ring. So much more romantic than a big, flashy stone.'

'Yes, we thought so, too,' Mike agreed,

smiling as he tucked his arm round Elizabeth's waist and kissed her tenderly, making her heart weep bitter tears. It was all for show, she knew, but when they were with Helen she saw a side of Mike that made her wish he could be like that more often. As it was, when they left the nursing home all his barriers went back up again.

She often wondered about the identity of the woman who had made him resolve never to let another woman near him. Whoever she had been, she must have hurt him badly. Perhaps he still cared for her, deep inside.

Her one consolation was that, since she had agreed to marry him, he had refrained from making intimate advances. He was giving her time to get used to the idea—as if that were possible. He never even tried to kiss her now, except when a show of affection was needed for someone else's benefit.

Not that she wanted him to kiss her. Just being with him so much was enough to keep her nerves in a state of constant upheaval. She was so aware of him that his slightest touch set her flesh alight with a fearful anticipation that made her feel ill, her heart pounding and her lungs constricted. She hated both herself and him because he had the power to affect her so deeply, in a way she knew was purely physical. He had turned her into a female animal, longing for his touch when her mind rejected the idea completely. She was beginning to dread the wedding.

*   *   *

On a breezy Sunday morning, Mike took Elizabeth and Bran down to the village near Belle Mer, to introduce her to the friend he intended to have as best man. Dave Harding. Apparently the two men often spent Sunday mornings out sailing. Perhaps now, Elizabeth thought, she would discover the identity of the redhead she had seen sailing with Mike.

Dave Harding lived in a big old house half hidden by trees, a rambling, untidy place with an air of cheerful neglect about it. Even inside it was untidy, towels and shoes lying around, and books in toppling piles. Dave matched the house. Big, bearded, full of bonhomie, he greeted Elizabeth warmly and gave her a smacking kiss on the cheek, laughing at Mike.

'Don't mind if I kiss the bride-to-be, do you?'

'So long as you only do it in my presence,' Mike replied with a smile. 'Oh, Peggy, come and meet Elizabeth.'

The redheaded girl had appeared in the open doorway whch led to the kitchen. She was younger than Elizabeth had thought, about sixteen, very slim and petite in tight jeans and sleeveless T-shirt as she regarded Elizabeth with mournful eyes.

'Hello,' Elizabeth said softly, realising that

93

she had probably just destroyed all the girl's romantic dreams about Mike.

'Hello,' Peggy returned, and bent to pet Bran as he padded across to say hello in his own way.

'A girl of few words, my daughter,' Dave said with heavy humour. 'Well, so you're the lady who's finally captured this old reprobate, are you? I've kept telling him it was time he settled down. Can't enjoy yourself all your life, you know, Mike. Got to accept responsibility some time.' A momentary sadness clouded his eyes. 'Seriously, though, I'm delighted for you both.'

For a moment the room was full of nuances Elizabeth didn't understand, then Mike punched his friend's arm in a matey way. 'Don't get serious, it doesn't suit you. Isn't it about time we got out on the water? The tide's about right.'

'Oh—yes, if Elizabeth doesn't mind.'

'No, not at all,' she replied.

'I won't be too long,' Mike promised, an arm round her shoulders as he kissed her cheek. Then he grinned at Peggy, said, 'See you at lunch,' and was gone.

Bran would have gone, too, except that Peggy had firm hold of his collar. 'You'd better shut the door,' she told Elizabeth. 'Otherwise he'll be off after them, getting in the way.'

Elizabeth closed the door and Peggy let the dog go. He bounded to the window, paws on the sill, head on one side as if wondering why he had been left behind. Beneath the trees, Elizabeth saw the two men making for the bay and the dinghies. Mike looked relaxed and at home. She hoped he might glance round, but he didn't; she found herself touching the place on her cheek where his lips had branded her yet again.

'I've got to get on,' said Peggy. 'Sit down, if you want.'

'What have you got to do?' Elizabeth asked.

The girl's gesture took in the muddled room. 'What does it look like?'

'May I help?'

Peggy shrugged, as if she didn't care one way or the other. 'Suit yourself.'

Her attitude was not calculated to be welcoming, but Elizabeth determined to stay and somehow break through the girl's sullen resentment. She helped Peggy clear the remains of breakfast, then set about the washing up while the girl tidied the living room and got out the vacuum cleaner, with Bran in and out between them wanting attention.

By that time, Elizabeth had got used to the dog and was becoming quite attached to him. He loved to be fondled and stroked, and only got over-exuberant when Mike took him out for an energetic run. The two of them would race and wrestle, tumbling about. Bran adored his master and hated to be without him.

'He'll be back soon,' Elizabeth promised the

dog, crouching to ruffle his ears and turn aside from the caress of a wet tongue. Laughing, she straightened and saw Peggy watching her from the doorway.

'Mike usually stays for lunch,' the girl said.

'Yes, so he told me,' Elizabeth replied. 'I gather your father invited us both today.'

Peggy was silent for a moment, as if puzzling over something. 'You mean . . . you *are* having lunch with us?'

'If you don't mind. I can help you get it ready, if you like. Didn't you want to go sailing today?'

'It's my turn to get the lunch ready,' Peggy replied. 'I'm not a very good cook, though.'

'Neither am I,' said Elizabeth with a grimace. 'Still, we'll see what we can do between us, eh?'

Slowly, she was breaking through Peggy's suspicion. The girl seemed pleased of some help and gradually the two of them transformed the living quarters into something resembling neatness.

Elizabeth wondered what had become of Dave's wife. Mike hadn't mentioned her, but framed photographs on the bookshelves showed Dave and Peggy with a pretty woman who must be Mrs Harding. Perhaps she was dead. Perhaps that was why Dave had suddenly choked up earlier. Elizabeth didn't like to ask in case her curiosity upset Peggy.

'I'll take Bran down to the harbour now,'

Peggy said when she had set the last vegetables on to cook. 'I always go and meet them. Will you stay and look after the food? I mean, you can come with me if you like, but . . .'

But you would rather have Mike to yourself for a few minutes, Elizabeth thought. 'No, I'll stay and make sure the pans don't boil dry,' she said lightly. 'You go. And tell them to get a move on, or the food will be spoiled.'

Half an hour later, when the aroma of roast pork was making her hungry, she glanced out of the living room window and saw Mike and Bran approaching with the Hardings. As she watched, Mike and Peggy burst out laughing over something Dave had said, and Mike threw an avuncular arm round Peggy's shoulders, his face alight in a way Elizabeth had seldom seen before.

Something twisted inside her, something that made her feel tender and yet excluded. Why couldn't he ever look at her like that, or laugh with such obvious enjoyment at something *she* said?

That lunch was a happy occasion, when it was easy to pretend that she was happily engaged to Mike Delaval. He seemed relaxed in those homely surroundings, with his friends. But when he looked at her there remained that shut-off expression in his eyes. It was Dave and Peggy who were lightening his spirits, plus a morning spent out with the waves and the breeze. It had nothing to do

97

with herself.

She chatted with Peggy about school, discovering that the girl loved her art classes best. Peggy talked with enthusiasm about prizes she had won with her paintings and drawings, and as soon as she had finished her apple pie she jumped up, wanting to show Elizabeth her folio.

'Dad and Mike will do the washing up,' she added. 'That's their part of the job.'

'That's right,' her father agreed. 'You girls go off and relax for half an hour. We'll get cleared up here. And Elizabeth . . . I'm grateful for your help. The place was turning into a pigsty.'

'I was only the assistant,' Elizabeth said. 'Peggy did most of it.' And she followed Peggy from the room, thinking that Mike with an apron on and a tea-towel in his hand would be a sight worth seeing.

Peggy's bedroom walls were covered in posters of pop stars, but her bed was neatly made and her things in order. Getting out a folder of her art work, she began to show them to Elizabeth, who was impressed.

'You're very talented,' she commented. 'Are you going to make a career out of it?'

'I hope so. I want to be a commercial artist. Maybe with an advertising agency in London.' The girl trailed a thin hand across the folder as she looked up through her lashes, her mouth awry. 'Will you forgive me?'

'For what?' asked Elizabeth in genuine surprise.

'I was sure I'd hate you,' Peggy explained. 'But you're not like the other one. *She* was a right snob! You should have seen the way she turned her nose up at everything when Mike brought her here. I was only a kid at the time, ten or eleven, but I hated her. You're different. You got stuck in and helped. The other one would have been scared of ruining her manicure.'

'And who,' Elizabeth said quietly, 'is "the other one"?'

'I can't remember her name. She was French. She—' Looking horrified, Peggy stared at her, blushing scarlet. 'Don't you know about her? Gosh, I'm sorry, Elizabeth. I was sure Mike would have told you. Not that you've got anything to worry about. She was ages ago.'

'She was Mike's girl-friend?' Elizabeth asked.

'They were engaged. Your ring's nice, but *she* had this huge emerald, big as an egg. I'm glad she found someone else. She wouldn't have liked Mike coming here. She'd have put a stop to that, you could tell. Even if he was unhappy for a while, he's got over that now. He's home again, and he's got you. So it's all worked out for—'

She was interrupted by a roar from the hall below. 'Peggy!' her father bellowed. 'Phone for

99

you. It's Jane.'

'Oops!' said Peggy. 'I'm supposed to be meeting her. 'Scuse me, Elizabeth.'

Left alone, Elizabeth wondered whether Peggy was quite as guileless as she appeared. Her mention of 'the other one' might have been an innocent slip, but it might equally have been meant as a dart to wound Elizabeth. Obviously Peggy had a teenage crush on Mike, poor girl. Elizabeth could understand her immature jealousy.

A short while later, Elizabeth and Mike took their leave of Dave and went out with Bran to the Land Rover, which Mike always used when he had the dog with him: Bran was much too rumbustious to be trusted in the Mercedes. The dog leapt into the back of the vehicle, panting as Elizabeth climbed to the passenger seat.

'I appreciate what you did today,' Mike said as they drove through the village and up the hill towards Belle Mer. 'They're struggling a bit, with Angela being away.'

'Angela?' she queried.

'Dave's wife. Her parents live up in Scotland. She doesn't see much of them, so she's taking an extended holiday.'

'Oh, I see. Somehow I thought . . .'

He shot her a guarded look. 'You thought what?'

'That she was dead. Just shows how wrong first impressions can be. I also assumed Peggy was suffering from a crush on you. That's probably true, but mainly she was anti-me because she was afraid I'd keep you away from her.'

'Then Peggy was wrong, too,' he said.

'You . . . never told me you'd been engaged before,' Elizabeth ventured.

'What?' He gave her a startled look and laughed shortly. 'Peggy's been chattering, has she? Don't tell me you thought you were the first woman in my life?'

'I'd have been a fool if I had. Are you going to tell me what happened?'

'When?'

'With your other fiancée!'

He glanced at her again with a tight, tell-nothing smile. 'She asked too many questions, that's what. Leave it be, Elizabeth. It's not important.'

But it *was* important, to her anyway, because she kept remembering how he had spoken so scathingly about love making a 'damn fool' of a man. Had that first engagement left wounds which had not yet healed?

The vehicle turned in through the gates of Belle Mer and took the curving rise to stop by the steps.

'Give Helen my regards,' said Mike. 'Tell her I'll see her this evening, unless I break my neck playing squash. By the way,—I've been meaning to ask you—What are you planning to wear next Saturday?'

'That's supposed to be a secret from the blushing groom,' said Elizabeth, disturbed by the reminder of how close the wedding had come. 'Something simple, I thought, especially if we're catching a plane straight after the ceremony. There won't be time to get changed.'

Reaching in the back pocket of his jeans for his wallet, he extracted a sheaf of notes. 'Have this. Get something nice.'

She recoiled as if he were offering her a spider. 'I don't need it. I've got savings of my own.'

'Don't be stupid!'

'I'm not being stupid,' she said dully. 'It's all too easy for you, Mike. I won't be bought.'

Putting the money away, he glared at her. 'Is that what that business with the ring was all about? You're too proud to take anything from me?'

'I don't *want* anything from you! You're doing enough. You're ensuring my aunt's peace of mind—that's what we agreed. Look, I'd better go or I'll be late for visiting hours. I'll see you this evening.'

Swiftly, she left the vehicle and ran up the steps to the imposing columned porch, only to halt as Mike called her name. He came after her with a determined look on his face, and suddenly she wanted to escape.

'Aren't you going to kiss me goodbye?' he

asked, pausing in front of her with eyes that taunted her. 'Six days from now we'll be man and wife. Do you begrudge your future husband a simple kiss?'

She swallowed the constriction in her throat, shivering as he lifted his hands to cup her face. How easily her flesh responded to him! Even though inches separated them she was vividly aware of his body and his long legs. Blue eyes burned into hers as he lowered his head, until she had to shut out the sight. His breath caressed her lips, and she felt the familiar tingle as her nerve-ends prepared for his kiss.

He held her there for endless moments, his mouth a whisper away from hers. Despite her efforts to remain unmoved, she trembled helplessly. Her hands spread across his shirt, enjoying the sensation of firm flesh through thin cotton. She began to think that if he didn't close the gap between their lips and release her from this terrible tension of longing, she would go mad.

'Don't want anything from me?' he murmured. 'Oh, you liar, Elizabeth. Oh, you liar!'

Her eyes flew open as he lifted his head and stepped away, watching her with a sardonic glint in his eye. 'But I can be patient,' he added. 'At least until next Saturday. Goodbye.'

Shaken by the feelings he had stirred inside her, she flung herself into the house and ran up to her room, muttering, 'I hate him, I hate him!' She rushed to her mirror and glared at her shiny-eyed, pink-cheeked reflection. *'Hate him!'* she repeated with all the venom she could muster. And in her head, mocking her, came the echo of Mike's words: 'Oh, you liar, Elizabeth. Oh, you liar!'

CHAPTER SIX

On the eve of her wedding, after paying her usual visit to her aunt, Elizabeth drove out to the airport to meet the flight from London, which was bringing her flatmates, Bettina and Lucille, for a weekend in Jersey. Her friends would accompany her to the register office and afterwards enjoy two days at Belle Mer.

The wedding was to be very simple; Elizabeth herself had decided that she wanted no big church affair. Mike would have the support of Dave and Peggy, and Elizabeth would have Bettina, Lu and her aunt— providing that when the time came the doctor felt that Helen could take the excitement. Since she had learned that her niece was to marry the 'wonderful' Mike Delaval, Helen's health had improved rapidly. She was determined to attend the ceremony, even though she would have to be in a wheelchair, with a couple of nurses standing by. The doctor had been amazed by her progress, though he had warned Elizabeth that it might not be a lasting effect. Care was still needed. No shocks, no upsets. Otherwise . . .

Elizabeth was all too well aware of the possibilities. Why else would she be going through with this farce of a marriage?

Lu and Bettina wanted to hear all about Mike. They complained that Elizabeth had been miserly with details about him, and now they were disappointed that she didn't even have a photograph of him to show them.

'We'll just have to wait until we see him tomorrow,' Bettina said as the three young women sat in the lounge at Belle Mer over drinks. 'And where are you going for your honeymoon?'

'I don't know,' said Elizabeth. 'No, honestly I don't. We'll be spending the first night in Paris, with his family. They were put out that he wasn't getting married in France and making a big splash, so we've compromised by letting them throw a dinner party for us. After that we'll go on somewhere. Mike's keeping the destination a secret even from me. But we shan't be away for long. I want to get Aunt Helen's rooms ready, in case she's allowed home soon.'

Lu, curled up in a chair with her feet tucked under her and her elfin face alight with mischief, said archly, 'If *I* were marrying a gorgeous man I don't think I'd take him home to live with *my* aunt!'

'It's more a case of her coming to live with us,' Elizabeth replied. 'Mike . . . is buying Belle Mer.'

'But doesn't he mind having your aunt here?' Bettina asked.

'No, not at all,' said Elizabeth. 'He's just as anxious to keep her happy as I am. He's really very fond of her.' That, at least, was true.

'You *are* lucky,' Lu told her. 'Rich, handsome, and nice to your family. I don't suppose he has any brothers available, does he?'

The girl-talk helped Elizabeth through an evening when she was aware of bridges burning behind her. Too late now to think of changing her mind, even if that were possible.

*　　　*　　　*

Her wedding day dawned with a slight sea-mist that soon rose to leave a warm, sun-drenched day just perfect for a wedding. June bride, Elizabeth thought with a sigh as Lu and Bettina fussed round making final adjustments to her outfit. It was a classic day dress the colour of rich dairy cream, and she had bought a neat straw hat to match, trimmed with a tiny eye-veil which was her one concession to bridal tradition. Her hair was fastened up with a few tendrils loose to soften the severe style, and she wore her plain gold necklet and bracelet. But beneath the hat's shadow her face looked pale and her eyes were haunted.

They were about to leave Belle Mer when a florist's van arrived bringing a lovely posy of roses for her, with corsages for Lu and Bettina. Elizabeth read the accompanying message with a sick emptiness at the pit of her stomach—'I'll be there, I promise,' it read. 'Mike.' But was it a promise or a threat? she wondered as her friends sighed over the romantic gesture and pinned their corsages to their pretty outfits.

Bettina drove the car in which they all went to the nursing home to join Helen, who actually looked better than Elizabeth felt. She was transported by ambulance in a wheelchair, with two nurses in attendance.

At the register office, Mike was waiting, with Dave and Peggy beside him. He wore a dark suit whose immaculate cut emphasised his height and broad-shouldered leanness, and Elizabeth felt her instincts respond as he regarded her with grave eyes.

Feeling as thought she were sleep-walking, she heard the words of the marriage ceremony. If only it could have been for real! If only Mike had been in love with her! He was not a bad man, nor always harsh. Somewhere inside him there must be tender feelings which a woman might reach, if she tried hard enough.

Man and wife. It was done, with a broad

gold wedding band on her finger to prove it. Mike turned to her, face sombre, eyes still, and bent to place a gentle kiss on the corner of her mouth. His lips felt like ice on her skin, chilling her to her soul.

Afterwards, she remembered vignettes of that morning's activities: her aunt in happy tears; Bettina and Lu expressing laughing jealousy; Dave giving her a smacking, prickly kiss and then Peggy actually hugging her; and Mike himself, a constant vibrant presence at her side. His hand beneath her arm felt possessive, but that cool reserve remained deep in his eyes despite his smiles.

Eventually they boarded a plane, leaving behind the friends who had come to the airport to see them off. Lu and Bettina waved merrily, looking forward to their weekend at Belle Mer. Dave and Peggy waved, too; they would be taking care of Bran while Mike was away.

As the plane taxied down the runway, Elizabeth stared out of the window to avoid looking at the man who was, unbelievably, her husband. 'Aunt Helen stood up to it well, don't you think?' she asked.

'She was fine,' he assured her. 'I was concerned about her, too, but she's tougher than she looks.'

'Maybe so.' She glanced in the general direction of his white shirt and grey silk tie. 'But I shall be happier when she's allowed to come home.'

'Not having second thoughts already, are you?' he asked sardonically.

'No,' Elizabeth replied. 'I just . . . I never imagined it would be like this when I got married.'

'The register office was your idea,' he reminded her. 'You could have had the white lace and orange blossom if you'd wanted.'

'I know.' What use was it trying to explain to him that she was not talking about the trimmings but about what lay between them? Mike wouldn't understand her longing for something other than a practical business agreement. She twisted her hands in her lap, touching the wedding band that bound her to a man who scorned the very notion of love. A level-headed, physical union might be fine for him, but more and more she was convinced that it wouldn't suit her, not at all.

*   *   *

By late afternoon they were circling to land at Paris. Below them, the Seine glinted as it snaked among grey buildings interspersed with the green of parks and gardens. Elizabeth glimpsed the Eiffel Tower in the distance, and then the plane was coming in to land. Soon she was being hustled into a taxi.

On a graceful road of tall houses which stood afoot behind railings and trees, the taxi stopped and Mike led his bride up steps to an elegant mansion. They were greeted by a svelte blonde who at first sight looked scarcely older than Mike. She wore her pale hair swept up to emphasise a long, slender neck, and though she was tall she was slim and gracious, dressed by some exclusive couturier.

'This is my aunt, Véronique Dupris,' Mike informed Elizabeth.

'How do you do,' Elizabeth said politely, holding out her hand, and the older woman laughed as if delighted.

'But she's charming, Jean-Michel,' she smiled. 'So English! My dear . . .' she pressed a scented cheek to Elizabeth's, 'you're welcome in my house. But you look tired. I, too, find flying quite exhausting. Take her up to your room, Jean-Michel—your usual room. I'll have someone bring your bags. And when you're ready we'll have coffee in the *salon*.'

The house was exquisite. High, elegant rooms opened from a marble-floored hall, full of Louis Quinze furniture and porcelain, like a miniature palace. Wrought iron delicate as lace formed a balustrade for the grand staircase which led to upper floors, where Mike conducted Elizabeth to a large bedroom whose window was heavily netted. A high, ornate ceiling presided over Turkish carpet and antique furniture, and a draped fourposter dominated the room, making Elizabeth look askance at its silken coverlet and plump bolsters.

'Your aunt seems very nice,' she chattered nervously. 'Is she married?'

'Divorced. This used to be my grandfather's residence, but Tante Véronique lives here now. There's also her brother, my uncle Anton Delaval and his wife, and their son Raoul and *his* wife, and *their* son—'

'Oh, stop!' Elizabeth cried.

Giving her a tight smile, Mike said, 'Have a rest. I'm going to talk to Tante Véronique. Business, I'm afraid.'

A manservant brought their cases and a maid arrived with coffee which she set down before beginning to unpack with swift efficiency. Sipping her coffee, Elizabeth stood by the window feeling as though she had been whisked to another world, where she could never belong. Even Mike seemed different; here he was Jean-Michel, a member of the rich and powerful Delaval family, and suddenly Elizabeth was afraid of him and everything he represented.

When the maid had gone, she took off the dress in which she had been married, loosened her hair and put a thin robe on top of her slip. She lay down on the high soft bed, thinking only to rest for a while and prepare herself for the ordeal of dinner with the Delavals. But with her eyes closed, the sound of traffic outside reminded her of London and the flat she had shared with Bettina and Lu. What were they doing now, back at Belle Mer? And how did her aunt feel after the stress of the day?

Almost asleep, she was startled by a child's high-pitched voice just outside her door, shouting '*Non! Maman, non!*' Before Elizabeth could move, the door swung wide open and a little dark-haired boy rushed in to dash across the room and squeeze himself into a corner by a bureau.

'Paul!' a stern female voice came from the doorway where stood a slender brunette in shirt and slacks of pale blue silk. She spoke rapidly in French, appearing to be apologising to Elizabeth, who understood no more than one word in five. The flow of words stopped and the two young women stared at each other, Elizabeth startled and embarrassed to be caught tousled with sleep. The stranger's eyes narrowed momentarily before her red mouth curved in a smile.

'You must be Elizabeth,' she said. 'You are the wife of Jean-Michel, *non?* You speak French?'

Still sitting on the bed, Elizabeth pushed back her tumbled hair. 'No, not much. I'm sorry.'

'It's nothing,' the woman said with a graceful little gesture. 'I am Marie-Clair. My husband is Raoul Delaval. He is cousin to Jean-Michel.'

'I'm pleased to meet you,' said Elizabeth,

slipping off the bed to shake hands.

From the corner, the child giggled nervously. Marie-Clair's lips tightened and she strode across to drag the boy out from his hiding place and speak to him angrily. He looked to be about four, a beautiful child with great brown eyes full of mischief.

'He is a bad boy,' Marie-Clair said. 'Please forgive him. He runs about this house as if it was a playground. I have told him he must not come in here again, not while his uncle Jean-Michel is here.'

'I really don't mind,' said Elizabeth, smiling at the child, who gave her a cheeky grin. 'He's lovely. Your son?'

Marie-Clair hesitated, then said, 'Yes. And how is Jean-Michel? Is he well?'

'Yes, he's fine.'

'I have not seen him for a long time,' Marie-Clair told her. 'He prefers his islands. Does he still know those strange people . . . what was their name—Harding?'

'Yes, he does.' Elizabeth was puzzled by the expression in eyes of a deep, unusual green set in a perfect face with porcelain-clear skin. On the surface Marie-Clair was all friendliness, but beneath there lurked a hint of animosity whose cause Elizabeth could not fathom.

'I must go,' Marie-Clair said abruptly. 'Come, Paul. Goodbye, Elizabeth. We will meet later.'

'I'll look forward to it. *Au revoir*, Paul.'

The little boy looked round, staring with great brown eyes. *"Voir,'* he replied as his mother hustled him from the room and closed the door.

Elizabeth remained where she was, puzzled by something she couldn't explain even to herself. She had a feeling that her meeting with Marie-Clair had been significant, but she couldn't imagine why.

Realising that it was after six and Mike might be back at any minute, she went into the adjoining bathroom and took a quick shower. Fortunately she was dressed apart from her dinner gown, wearing her wrap and sitting at the mirror applying make-up when Mike came in. She ignored him, continuing to stroke mascara on to her lashes.

'All right?' he asked.

'Fine,' Elizabeth replied.

'We'll go down about eight,' he said. 'I'll just have a shower.' And to her surprise—and relief—he shut himself into the bathroom without even coming near her.

For that evening she had brought her one good evening dress—a black chiffon whose fitted top was held by thin straps, with a floaty skirt of cocktail length. She stepped into it and was struggling with the zip when the bathroom door opened. She swung round to see Mike wearing only a towel tucked round his waist, his tanned legs and chest still gleaming with dampness.

114

Elizabeth froze, flushing hotly at the sight of athletic muscles rippling under bronzed skin shadowed with a growth of dark hair. From the gleam in his eyes she guessed he was aware of her embarrassment, and amused by it.

'Want some help?' he asked.

'No, I can manage, thank you.' Turning away from him, she tugged awkwardly at the zip, her arms twisted behind her. The thing was stuck.

'Here, let me,' said Mike from right behind her, removing her hands from the zip and putting his own hands in their place. His fingers against her flesh made it quiver so much she wanted to wrench away. 'You've got it caught in the material,' he told her. 'Hold still!'

Elizabeth did so, holding her breath and steeling herself not to react to the intimacy of his touch on her spine. He reached inside her dress to keep it straight while he gently pulled the zip down a fraction and said, 'Got it.' Then with maddening slowness he closed the zip and let his fingers trail lightly across her shoulderblade.

Shivering, she moved away. 'Thank you.'

'You're welcome,' he said. 'What are husbands for?'

She glanced round to say something that died on her lips as he removed the towel and began to rub himself down as if she weren't there. She caught a hint of mockery in his eyes as he saw her dismay, and she swung away to

115

stare out of the netted window. Her fingers curled tightly into her palms in an effort to stop the desire to touch him.

Behind her, he moved about the room opening drawers and, presumably, getting dressed. 'Oh, by the way,' he said, 'I phoned the nursing home to let Helen know we arrived safely. Apparently she's doing fine—stood up to the ordeal very well, according to the nurse.'

'I'm glad to hear it,' said Elizabeth, wishing she could breathe properly. 'It was kind of you to think of it. She probably would be anxious.'

His feet made no sound on the carpet and suddenly he was beside her, holding a small flat jewellery box for her to see. 'This is for you.'

Surprised, she glanced at his enigmatic face. 'What is it?'

'It's a wedding present.'

He stood very close to her, his powerful torso still naked and giving off a heady scent that rose with his warmth to engulf her. A glance told Elizabeth that at least he had put on a pair of briefs, but she still felt breathless and lightheaded.

Inside the box lay a necklace of glittering diamonds, with a matching bracelet. She stared at the jewels, her throat dry. She had vowed not to take anything from him, but from the way he stood tensely beside her she guessed that any argument might provoke him into a temper that could lead anywhere—probably to that wide, soft bed.

'I want you to wear them tonight,' he said, lifting the sparkling necklace to lay it round her throat, where it felt cool and heavy as he fastened the catch and then slipped the bracelet round her wrist. Her flesh tingled where he touched her and she was assailed by his live, near-naked warmth so close to her that he drugged all her senses.

Looking down at the bracelet, she touched the necklace, thinking that she had never owned anything so beautiful. But the glitter of the diamonds marked her as Jean-Michel Delaval's possession, and that frightened her.

'I suppose we have to put on a show,' she muttered. 'You wouldn't want me to disgrace you.'

He caught his breath. His hands shot out to fasten on her shoulders and shake her, tipping her head back so that through wide, terrified eyes she saw him glowering. 'That's not—' he began, but the fury in him changed subtly and with a groan he threw his arms round her, bending to kiss her.

She turned her head aside and he buried his lips in the hollow of her throat, his arms tightening convulsively to press her closer to his body. Elizabeth's mind beat with panic as her hands encountered his naked flesh, trying to push him off.

'Mike!' she breathed frantically. 'Don't—

117

there's no time. It's nearly eight. We'll be late.'

'Who cares?' he growled, lifting his head to find her lips, but again she evaded him, pushing at him, twisting her head from side to side.

'You'll get lipstick all over you. It took me ages to get it right. Please, Mike!'

His efforts ceased and he moved a little away, a hand flat against her throat stroking down to her shoulder. His glance followed the movement as if to learn every curve and hollow of her. 'I want you,' he said hoarsely. 'Do you know how difficult it's been, keeping my distance this past month? Now you're mine, and I can't wait much longer.'

'Later, though,' she breathed, hoping he couldn't hear the fear in her voice. 'We mustn't keep your family waiting.'

He stepped back, removing himself from her with a visible effort, and gave her a look like blue lightning. 'I wish to God we'd been able to avoid even coming here. But tomorrow we'll get away on our own.'

As he began to dress, Elizabeth sat at the mirror making final adjustments to her face and hair. Covertly she watched as Mike donned a crisp white shirt, black trousers and bow tie. He combed his hair into unusual neatness before slipping on the black dinner jacket he had worn at The Cliff, so long ago, when she had been stupid enough to be bewitched by him. Everything was different

118

now. If she had realised that being married to him would fill her with suffocating panic every time he came near, she might not have gone through with it. But she had been forced to go through with it, for her aunt's sake. Somehow she must find a way to bear it.

'Haven't you finished titivating yet?' he asked as she tweaked a curling wisp of hair at her brow. 'I expect you're nervous. Don't be—my family will be delighted with you.'

Elizabeth glanced at him, surprised by his sensitivity to her mood. 'This is all very strange to me. I don't even speak French.'

'Well, most of them speak English, so that's no problem,' he said. 'Elizabeth, hurry up! I thought you were anxious not to keep them waiting.'

She stood up, fluffing out her skirt, her heartbeat unsteady. 'How many of them will there be? At least I've met three who won't be strangers. Or will Paul be in bed by now?'

He was reaching for his watch and she saw his slight pause, but he had his back to her so his expression was hidden. 'Paul?' he said carefully. 'When did you meet him?'

'Earlier. He came bursting in here, running away from his mother.'

'You met Marie-Clair, too?' asked Mike, still in that careful voice, still keeping his face averted.

'Yes, I did. Why, what's wrong?'

He turned then, smiling with his mouth but

not his eyes. 'Nothing at all. So what did you think of them?'

'I didn't really have time to judge. Marie-Clair is very beautiful, isn't she? And Paul is gorgeous, though he seemed to be a bit of a handful.'

'Yes, and fortunately he should be well out of the way tonight, being looked after by his nanny. Small undisciplined children can wreak havoc at dinner parties. Shall we go?'

And so Elizabeth, on her husband's arm, was taken down to meet his family, with her stomach a-churn with nerves.

The great *salon*, its walls done in striped silk to match the upholstery, held what at first seemed a bewildering crowd of people. The men all wore dinner jackets and the women were elegantly gowned. Slowly, Elizabeth picked out one from another.

There was Tante Véronique, blonde and slender in midnight blue; Oncle Anton, still a very handsome man in his fifties, though his wife was rather plump. Their son Raoul had inherited his father's dark good looks plus his mother's tendency to overweight. He sported a bandit moustache and had dark, slumbrous eyes that Elizabeth found too bold for her comfort. She had the impression that Raoul and Mike didn't like each other much.

Marie-Clair, Raoul's wife, looked stunning in a black satin skirt and a strapless blouse of white lace flounces, with emeralds round her neck and in her ears, almost matching her eyes. She must favour those green stones, for she wore another emerald on her right hand— a massive stone worth a fortune.

From elsewhere in the city had come the remaining Delavals—Oncle Richard, a quiet, unassuming man with a lovely wife and twin daughters aged eighteen; each stunning twin had brought with her an adoring escort. And there was also an old lady whom everyone addressed as Madame Claude; she, apparently, was Mike's great-aunt, the matriarch of the family.

All of them seemed pleased to welcome a new Madame Delaval into their midst. They took pains to make Elizabeth feel at home.

Eventually the company moved into the dining room. A long polished table gleamed in candlelight, with flowers massed along the centre. Elizabeth and Mike were given pride of place either side at the end of the table where Madame Claude presided. The old lady was slightly deaf and her English not very good. During the meal, when she made comments to Elizabeth, Mike had to translate the answer, shouting into the old lady's ear.

Perhaps because of the fine wines that accompanied the meal, Elizabeth began to find she was enjoying herself. On her left, Anton Delaval kept chiming in with dry remarks which made everyone laugh, with the exception of Madame Claude, who couldn't hear him properly. She kept glaring round the table, saying peremptorily, *'Quoi? Quoi?'*

'She sounds like a duck,' Anton murmured to Elizabeth, making her laugh out loud, only to sober suddenly as she saw Mike watching her with a possessive hunger that brought her out in a sweat. *Later,* she had promised him, and the evening was slipping away.

When Madame Claude decided it was time for the ladies to leave the men to talk over their cognac, Elizabeth slipped upstairs to repair her make-up. She stood by the part-open window in the bedroom, gulping in the fresh night air and wishing she had not indulged in so much wine. It had helped to relax her, but now she felt muzzy and couldn't think clearly. If she made a fool of herself, Mike would be furious. Soon it would be time for bed. Oh God, suppose he came looking for her!

Knowing that too long an absence would cause curiosity, she forced herself out of the bedroom and made her way slowly back to the high main hall. The lacy wrought-iron formed a balustrade for a curved gallery which lay in shadow over the marble floor and steep sweep of stairs. Elizabeth paused in the friendly twilight, trying to compose herself for a return to the *salon.*

While she stood there, the *salon* door opened. Laughter and conversation surged briefly out before Mike appeared and closed the door. He was making for the stairs, probably coming to find her.

'Jean-Michel!'

The urgent whisper from somewhere below Elizabeth made Mike stop and glance along the hall.

'Jean-Michel!' the whispered plea came again.

Elizabeth peered over the balustrade to where, at the back of the darkened hall, by an open doorway into an unlit room, Marie-Clair's white blouse showed up in the darkness. She extended a slender bare arm to beckon Mike across to her. Elizabeth saw him hesitate, then he slowly walked towards Marie-Clair.

The lovely young woman laid a hand on his shirt-front, her face lifted as she spoke in rapid, anguished French. He replied in the same language, so quietly that even if Elizabeth had understood she would not have been able to hear what was said.

'Jean-Michel!' Marie-Clair kept saying, edging ever closer to him. Her hands slid up his jacket, pale against the black fabric. 'Ah, Jean-Michel!'

Hardly believing her senses, Elizabeth seemed to stop breathing as Marie-Clair's hands locked behind Mike's neck. A stray gleam of light brought a flash of green from the emerald on her finger. *'Je t'aime!'* she cried. *'Je t'aime,* Jean-Michel!'

Even Elizabeth's schoolgirl French could translate that. Next second, to her sick horror, Mike had pulled Marie-Clair into his arms, his dark head bent over hers as he kissed her passionately.

Elizabeth turned and fled, hot tears bursting from her eyes. All at once she understood everything, though it had taken her a long time to translate the clues. All the pieces fitted— Marie-Clair's tension in the bedroom earlier; Mike's guardedness when Elizabeth mentioned his cousin's wife and child; Raoul's covert hostility and Peggy, chattering about 'the other one' who had an engagement emerald 'as big as an egg'. Marie-Clair must have kept that ring. She still wore it. And, whatever had happened to break up her relationship with Mike, she still loved him—the echo of her impassioned cry hurt Elizabeth's ears.

And Mike? Oh, yes, he had been hurt, but in his heart he had always kept a place for Marie-Clair. He could never love anyone else. Was he even now regretting his enforced marriage? Was he holding his lost love in his arms, kissing her and assuring her that he felt nothing for the girl who was now his wife?

CHAPTER SEVEN

With the room in darkness but for the faint glow from street-lamps outside, Elizabeth sat crumpled in a chair by the part-open window. Wild thoughts ran through her head; plans to pack her bags and escape; ideas about rushing down to confront Mike and his paramour. What would they do now—have a passionate affair until their respective marriages could be dissolved? Or had this been going on all through Marie-Clair's marriage to Raoul? Would it just continue?

When the door opened she sat with her hands clenched, her head near bursting as she saw Mike's tall figure outlined against the light from the hallway.

'Why are you sitting in the dark?' he asked as casually as if nothing had happened.

'Leave it!' Elizabeth cried as he reached for the light switch. His hand dropped and he came into the room, closed the door and became a dark figure among shadows as he advanced on her.

She shot to her feet, trembling. 'Don't touch me!'

'What?' He stopped dead in surprise a few feet away, and now she wished he had put the light on, so that she could see his face. 'What's wrong with you?'

She couldn't possibly tell him. He would only lie about it, or—far worse—be honest and admit that he loved Marie-Clair. Elizabeth couldn't bear to hear him do either. 'Nothing's wrong,' she croaked through a throat thick with tears.

'Don't lie to me, Elizabeth!' he rasped.

'I'm not lying! Go away. Leave me alone!'

Through the shadows, she fancied she saw his teeth flash in a snarl. He reached for her, but she backed away, sickened by the thought of his touching her.

'Elizabeth . . .' he said warningly.

'Stay away from me!'

A cut-off cry escaped her as he lunged and caught her wrist in bruising fingers, saying through his teeth, 'Now listen to me . . .' He swung her round against him, his free arm circling her waist.

'*You* listen!' she shot at him. 'I married you to protect my aunt. You've got what you want—you've got Belle Mer and a clear conscience. But that's all you'll get from me, Mike!'

'Yes, I had a feeling you were planning something like that,' he said with disgust. 'But it won't work, Elizabeth. You're my wife!'

'Only in name,' Elizabeth choked, horrified by the way his nearness weakened her resolve. Her only defence was outright attack, as wounding as she could make it. 'If you try to make love to me, I—I'll fight you off. I just

126

can't pretend any longer.'

His arm hardened, threatening to stop her breathe. 'Pretend?' he said in a fierce whisper. 'Who are you kidding?'

'It's true! Every time you come near me I feel ill—physically ill!'

With an exclamation of rage, he released her and she crumpled back into the chair, her hands to her face.

'That really is a pity,' Mike said, his voice hoarse, 'because I'm going to be near you from now on. We'll just see how long you can keep it "in name only."'

'For ever, if necessary!' she flung at him, and recoiled as he swooped on her, dragging her to her feet and back into his arms, a hand round her jaw forcing her to lift her face as he kissed her with brutal passion.

She fought him desperately, knowing that if he went on holding her she would melt against him. Suddenly he bent and swept her feet from under her to carry her to the bed.

'Mike, no!' she begged. 'Don't! Please!'

'No?' he snarled, depositing her on yielding softness and flinging himself down half on top of her, a crooked knee preventing her from kicking. His elbows pinioned her shoulders and his hands locked round her head. In the shadows, his smile was the coldest thing she had ever seen.

'No?' he repeated softly, tauntingly, and bent his mouth to hers with sensuous purpose, kissing her taut lips coaxingly. Little flicks of his tongue sent sparks along all her nerves.

She tried to remain rigid, but her body came alive to the weight of him against her. Undeniable responses flowed through her as her lips softened under his, allowing his subtle invasion. She knew his tenderness was pretended, but still her senses all reacted to him and she wondered if, even now, she might break through his shell and make him forget Marie-Clair.

Without her willing it, her arms crept round him. Her resistance had vanished. She was again the yearning female, longing for a completion and yet fearing it. Perhaps she had been wrong. Perhaps instead of fighting with him she should fight *for* him, with all the weapons at her disposal. He was her husband and he wanted her. As she wanted him.

Or was it Marie-Clair who had roused him to a pitch which he now wished Elizabeth to assuage?

He lifted his head and looked down at her, his expression lost in darkness. 'Make you ill, do I?' he breathed. 'Maybe you should see a doctor, Elizabeth. I'd be fascinated by his diagnosis of your present state.'

Her hopes fled, leaving her cold and ashamed. 'I hate you,' she muttered. 'I hate you!'

His laugh cut her like a knife to the heart as he rolled away from her and stood up, straightening his dinner jacket. 'Don't fight it, Elizabeth. I told you we were fated for each other. We'll see which one of us can hold out longest!'

Without haste, he made for the door and opened it. 'I'll tell them you don't feel well— too much wine, and wedding night nerves. See you soon.'

In the darkness after the door had closed, Elizabeth sat up, wanting to scream out loud with rage. Her fist thudded into the pillow, but the next second she threw herself down and wept helplessly, berating herself for her weakness. Jean-Michel Delaval was a devil who knew too much about women. He had no heart because he had long ago given it to someone else. *That* was what hurt most—that Marie-Clair had been able to reach him where to Elizabeth he remained shuttered and barred.

*   *   *

She slept heavily, dreamlessly, eventually waking as someone drew back the curtains, letting sunlight pour in through heavy net curtains. A smiling maid bade her, *'Bonjour, madame,'* and as Elizabeth struggled to sit up, rubbing her eyes, the maid placed a breakfast tray across her lap.

There was no sign of Mike, except for an indentation in the pillow next to Elizabeth, which proved that he had slept beside her even if she hadn't been aware of it. The wine must have drugged her, she thought. Even now her head felt thick. But all too clearly she remembered the previous night, when her naïve hopes for some sort of happiness had been crushed by Mike's derision.

The coffee slid down like nectar; the warm croissants were delicious with butter melting on them. On a breeze through the open window, the sound of Paris church bells came floating over the hum of traffic.

Having finished her breakfast, she set the tray aside and was about to get out of bed when the door swung open and Mike was there, casual in blue slacks and open-necked shirt. Elizabeth scrambled back into bed, drawing the duvet to cover her sheer nightgown. Her sea-green eyes fixed on her husband's face as she tried to read his mood.

He seemed relaxed, even cheerful, though it was a forced cheerfulness which failed to disguise his underlying tension. 'Well, good morning at last,' he said, strolling to lean on one of the draped posts at the foot of the bed. 'I thought you were going to sleep all day. Not that it's done my reputation any harm—the family appear to think my ardour exhausted you. I thought it best not to tell them you were merely paralytic with their good wine.'

Deciding not to rise to these sallies, Elizabeth said, 'Will you pass me my wrap,

130

please?'

'Of course.' He tossed the garment to her and watched her slide her arms into it. 'Though I don't know why you're suddenly so modest. When I came in last night, you'd kicked the covers right off. That's a very fetching nightgown, what little there is of it. Be grateful I managed to contain myself.'

Face burning, she slid carefully out of bed, keeping the wrap well round her and avoiding his eyes.

'I just came to tell you we'll be leaving in an hour,' he said.

'Oh?' she replied dully. 'Where are we going?'

'You'll find that out when we get there. I think you'll like it. We'll be all on our own at last. Won't that be romantic?'

The slamming door told her he had gone, and only then did she glance at the space where he had been, her heart aching. Did he really have to keep needling her? Didn't he know that she was already so emotionally bruised that she was defenceless?

Nothing seemed to matter any more. She felt very calm, resigned to her fate. As she took a shower she told herself that Mike had finally destroyed the tender feelings which had been growing inside her almost unnoticed. Those tiny shoots might have flowered into love, if only he had taken care of them. Instead, he kept attacking them with poison.

She wondered if it was Paris which had made him extra cruel. Or was it being so near to the unattainable Marie-Clair? Yes, that was more like it—Marie-Clair had revived feelings in him which he had thought dead, and now he was angry because he had tied himself to Elizabeth.

Neither Marie-Clair nor Raoul was in evidence when at last Elizabeth and Mike took their leave of the rest of his family and drove south out of Paris beneath brilliant June sunshine. Not far from the city, they paused for lunch before travelling on along the beautiful Loire valley with its great Renaissance châteaux, its vineyards and its orchards. Elizabeth watched the garden of France unfold before her, but its lush beauty was tainted by her depression. She felt like an empty shell, as though her heart had died inside her. The future stretched ahead bleak and cheerless.

Mike hardly spoke to her, except to point out places of interest. He, too, must be feeling pretty drear, she thought, having to carry on this farce of a honeymoon when the woman he really loved was back in Paris.

Where were they going—to some castle hotel, or one of the Delaval country homes? Not that it mattered. Nothing mattered.

The long light evening was still bright with sunlight when Mike turned off the main road on to a country lane running between meadows and woods, past little villages. Eventually he pulled on to a small car park beside an *auberge* which had evidently once been a mill. Now it provided shelter for visitors and travellers. Its rambling rooms stretched beneath a stepped roof. A stream ran by in a series of waterfalls where trees bent to admire their reflections in pools rippled by fish.

'Our honeymoon hotel,' Mike said in a toneless voice.

Elizabeth glanced at the charming old building, all angles and leaded windows, with ivy and flowering creepers trailing up its walls.

'I thought you'd like it,' said Mike.

Elizabeth turned empty eyes to his. 'Did you? Did you ever actually consider whether I'd like any of this? I'm not a person to you, Mike. I'm just a means of reclaiming Belle Mer without too much strain on your conscience.'

'You knew that,' he reminded her.

Sighing heavily, she looked down at the hands clasped in her lap. 'So I did. I just didn't realise what it would mean. It's not too late to—'

'Oh, yes it is,' he broke in, his voice hard. 'Much too late. We may as well make the best of it. That ceremony was legal, in case you hadn't realised it. Besides, I still own Belle Mer. Or had you forgotten that?'

Before she could reply, he had left the car and was striding to remove their luggage from the boot. She sat still, staring unseeingly at the trees and the stream, the sight wavering through tears. So he found his wedding vows binding, did he? What about the 'love, honour and cherish' bit?

Climbing from the car, she stretched her stiff legs. Appetising aromas drifted from the inn, and in the quietness of the evening birds sang sweetly above the soft rush of the waterfalls. It was a lovely spot which, in any other circumstances, Elizabeth would have found enchanting.

Their room nestled beneath a sloping roof, with a shower room adjoining it. The furniture was unpretentious and a hand-sewn patchwork quilt covered the wide, soft bed, giving the place a country charm all its own. The sight of the bed made Elizabeth's panic return, but Mike remained distant, like a polite stranger.

The cosy dining room was softly lit, the windows open to the night air and the sound of the stream. Despondent, Elizabeth picked at her trout in wine sauce, hearing the laughter and low-voiced conversation of other guests.

'I'll call the nursing home again later,' said Mike.

'Yes, fine,' she replied listlessly, and flinched as he reached across the table to grasp her wrist, making her look up to see anger flash in his blue eyes.

'For God's sake!' he breathed. 'I'm doing everything I can to please you. What else do you want? You went into this with your eyes open. I'm doing my part the best way I know how. Couldn't you show a little enthusiasm? You were bright enough with Oncle Anton last night.'

'I found your uncle very amusing,' she replied. 'And quite charming. Perhaps if you tried the same tactics it might help.'

He tossed her wrist away from him and sat glowering at her through his lashes. 'I thought we established there'd be no need for games like that, not between us. We had an agreement.'

'And *you* dictated the terms,' she reminded him. 'It might have worked if I'd been a computer, but I'm not—I'm a human being. A woman.'

'I'm aware of that,' he said, his glance flicking over her with a cool arrogance which was in itself an insult.

'Yes, and that's all I mean to you, isn't it?' Elizabeth muttered. 'Just a warm, soft shape. You seem to forget I have thoughts, and feelings.'

His mouth tightened in a brief grimace. 'I was under the impression that you were one of those rare females who used her head for something other than wearing hats. Now, all of a sudden, you've gone feminine on me. Your behaviour's illogical, you know that? The terms of our agreement still stand—your aunt stays at Belle Mer, and you become my wife.

My *wife*, Elizabeth.'

'I am your wife,' she said bitterly. 'You've got a piece of paper to prove it. And what have I got?—a husband who doesn't believe in love.' Or so he says, her mind added. Actually, what I have is a husband who is in love with another woman.

A corner of his mouth turned up in a wry smile. 'Is that what all this is about? I thought we agreed we'd have no emotional nonsense.'

'You agreed it, not me.' She glanced round the dining room, realising that their quarrel was in danger of attracting attention. 'Oh, what's the point of talking about it? I'm tired. I'm going up to the room.'

Beyond the leaded window in the eaves, trees sighed and the stream chuckled to itself. Elizabeth lay wide-eyed, watching the stippling of reflected moonlight on the slope of the ceiling. Mike was right, of course—she had agreed to his terms for this crazy marriage and now she must live with it, one way or another. But she had not realised how much it would hurt to know that Mike loved someone else. She could not bear the thought of his making love to her without being in love with her. But that was, as he had said, illogical female thinking. Too late, she understood why she had always stopped short in previous relationships—because, for her, loving and lovemaking could not be separated.

When eventually Mike came in, she lay

quietly as if asleep, her back turned to the room. She heard him take a shower and a short while later the shower room light clicked out, leaving only dappled moonlight. Mike came softly across to the bed and slipped beneath the single sheet, his weight an alien presence beside her.

She prayed that he would just go to sleep, as he had the previous night. For her there was no wine-induced oblivion to aid her now: she was wide awake, tinglingly aware of his live warmth, and more unhappy than she would have dreamed was possible.

A tear slid down her cheek into the plump pillow. Was this desolation to be her lot for the rest of her life?

She stiffened as Mike turned over towards her, and his hand slid up her arm.

'Still awake?' he asked softly.

'Mm,' she replied, not trusting herself to speak, but the catch in her voice was enough. He lifted himself on to one elbow, forcing her to turn on to her back.

He touched her face, feeling the wetness of her tears. 'Why are you crying?'

'Oh, what do you care?' she said wretchedly.

'Elizabeth . . . I'm trying to understand; but I really can't. You agreed—'

'Will you stop saying that?!' she muttered with gritted teeth, tears rolling down her face. 'I know I agreed—because you didn't give me any choice. You blackmailed me into this. Now

137

you expect me to enjoy it?'

'I assumed you'd carry on sniping at me the way you always have,' he said. 'But that sort of relationship can be stimulating. I don't understand what's happened to you recently. Are you worrying about your aunt? Do you want to go home?'

A stifled sob escaped her, half despair and half laughter, and she felt his puzzlement in the way he gently stroked her face and hair. Oddly enough, his touch comforted her. She remembered how his kisses could sweep her away on a tide of euphoria that made her forget everything else.

'I wish you'd tell me,' he whispered, his breath brushing her cheek as he bent over her, touching his lips to hers softly.

'Oh, Mike!' Elizabeth sobbed, flinging her arms round him, to discover with a little shock of surprise that he was naked. But by then it was too late; she needed the comfort of his arms around her. As his mouth met hers in a deep, possessive kiss her head seemed to explode with coloured lights. Sensation surged through her body, making her strain against him.

'I want you,' he muttered. 'God, how I want you! Elizabeth—'

The words scorched her and she wished he could have said 'I love you,' even if it was a lie. But there were no more words, only the mounting heat in him. His urgency turned

138

him into a harsh, demanding stranger in the darkness of the room. At first Elizabeth feared the need she sensed in him, but soon she was swept up on the tide herself. Her whole being became a mass of physical sensation as he touched, kissed and caressed her, until nothing mattered but that he should soothe the terrible ache inside her.

Her ears roared as the wildfire engulfed her and he claimed her for his own. He took her swirling upward, straining for the topmost peak where suddenly there was sunlight and release. Her body loosened with fulfilment as Mike shuddered against her and together they came spiralling down from the heights.

Reality returned to her slowly, making her despair of herself. She had reached out to him blindly, no longer caring that he felt nothing for her. Once again, her body had turned traitor. His weight seemed to be crushing her as he lay recovering his breath. She wanted to throw him off, to run and scrub herself in penance for her weakness.

When she shifted uncomfortably, he eased away from her, kissing her cheek. 'I always knew it would be good with you,' he said, and sighed contentedly. Within seconds, she could tell from his breathing that he was asleep.

Asleep! Just like that, after the most shattering experience of her life. Couldn't he have held her a little longer? She had needed his comfort and he had said he wanted to understand. Or had he said that just to soften her and make her compliant to his driving desires? For him it had been just another encounter. She had wanted to talk to him; when she reached for him she had been reaching for reassurance, but in his mind only one thing had predominated—his own need.

Now the truth came to her with bitter clarity: it had all started as a game, a battle of wits that had excited her both mentally and physically; if it had gone on that way then she might have made use of him as he made use of her. Unfortunately, somewhere along the way, she had fallen in love with him. It was no longer a game, but painfully real. Once she had said that she wanted nothing from him, but now she knew that she longed desperately for the one thing he could not give her—she wanted his love.

*　　　*　　　*

He woke her by singing in a melodic baritone that mingled with the sound of the shower. At least *he* sounded happy, Elizabeth thought sourly as she sat up, aching in every muscle. She felt soiled and bitter, almost hating Mike for taking her precious gift and then casually falling asleep as if her offering had meant little to him. But still part of her was glad that he had needed her, if only physically.

Holding the sheet to cover her, she

straightened her tousled hair as the shower cut off and Mike stepped into the bedroom, dripping, naked and totally unabashed to find her watching him. She couldn't turn away; her eyes drank in the sight of his perfect male form, all tanned but for the area covered by bathing trunks. Her throat felt thick as he smiled at her and continued to towel his hair.

'Sleep well?' he asked, finally draping the damp towel round his waist. 'I did. Must be the country air.'

'Must be,' Elizabeth echoed.

'Or something,' he added with a look that made her feel hot. The memory of last night's intimacy lay between them, shocking and shaming in the morning light. Her expression brought him to the bed, where he sat down beside her, holding her shoulders, frowning a little. 'I was in too much of a hurry, I know. Forgive me. Next time it will be better.'

'Will it, Mike?' she asked huskily. 'Better in what way? Will I stop feeling used and sick at myself?'

His fingers bit deeper into her flesh as he searched her eyes, his frown increasing. 'Is that the way you feel?'

'What did you expect?'

A breath of anger exploded from him as he whirled away and grabbed his clothes. He shut himself into the shower room, leaving Elizabeth trembling on the verge of more useless tears. With an effort she pulled herself together and climbed out of bed to pull on her robe. She went to lean in the open window, watching a duck waddle from beneath a shrub to the edge of the stream, with five tiny ducklings piping after her. The sight made her smile sadly to herself. Whatever the follies of humans, nature just carried on.

She glanced round as Mike emerged from the shower room dressed in jeans and close-fitting T-shirt, his face shuttered and his eyes veiled.

'Have it your way, then,' he said. 'I never yet forced myself on an unwilling woman and I'm damned if I'll start with you, however much you provoke me. But understand this, Elizabeth—if it's to be an open marriage, I'll go my own way without questions from you. I'm going for a walk now. I'll be back for breakfast in half an hour. You can join me or not, as you please.' He made for the door, where he turned to add, 'And we might as well save ourselves the embarrassment of prolonging this so-called honeymoon. You can pack the bags. We'll be leaving after breakfast.'

CHAPTER EIGHT

Waking to the sound of seagulls, Elizabeth lay with an arm across her eyes as she prepared for the day ahead. Over five weeks had passed since she and Mike returned to Belle Mer. Both of them had been living in a kind of limbo, but today that must alter: her aunt was coming home.

She wondered sadly how so much time could have gone by with no change in the deadlock between her and Mike. Probably it happened because she rarely saw him. With the tourist season in full swing he spent long hours at his office, rarely returning home until late in the evening. A couple of times he had not come home at all, but when she tackled him about it all she got was a fierce look and the comment, 'That's my affair.'

'Affair' was probably the right word. Many times she had cried herself to sleep thinking of him with someone else. Of course he found other company; that was what he had meant about going his own way. A man as virile and attractive as Mike would not wait long before some woman came smiling to ease his loneliness. And who could Elizabeth blame but herself? But if she wept at night, when morning came she resumed the polite uninterest which had become second nature to her. However much she hurt, she had too much pride to show it. If Mike suspected how she really felt, he would only pour scorn and wound her further.

Only towards her aunt did he show any warmth.

Two or three times a week he made a point

of accompanying Elizabeth to the nursing home where Helen was growing stronger every day. For the visiting hour, he and Elizabeth acted the part of a happy couple. At least he cared enough about Helen not to trouble her with doubts about the state of her niece's marriage, and for that Elizabeth was grateful. There were times, however, when she was almost jealous of her aunt's easy relationship with Mike.

Her one consolation was the company of Bran, who had formed an attachment to her that made him follow her everywhere. With Mike absent for most of the day, Elizabeth took the dog for long walks, often ending up at the big house in the village where Peggy was glad of some help with the chores. She was on holiday from school now, still playing woman of the house in her mother's prolonged absence.

*   *   *

Despite a strange reluctance to move, Elizabeth forced herself out of bed. She and Mike now occupied the master suite. It still contained the two beds—if Ben and Helen had been more comfortable sleeping separately, the same applied to Elizabeth and her husband, though for a different reason. Often she would be in bed when Mike came in, and in the mornings he always rose first to take a swim before starting the day. In the confines of the master suite, by tacit consent, they avoided each other as much as was possible.

Locking herself into the bathroom, she took a cool shower and let her hands rest on the flatness of her stomach. For the past two weeks she had been telling herself that many things could disrupt a woman's cycle—emotional upheaval, changes of lifestyle. That was all it was. It couldn't be anything else: Mike had only made love to her once.

But as each day passed, in her heart she became more sure that everything was perfectly normal—for a woman who was pregnant.

An impatient knock on the door made her jump, as if her thoughts were audible.

'Hurry up!' Mike called. 'I don't want to be late.'

Elizabeth shut off the water and, wrapped in a towelling robe, went into the bedroom. Mike stood by the window looking out across the garden. He was dressed only in blue trunks, with a towel slung round his neck, his dark hair sticking up in wild peaks, still wet from the pool. As always, the sight of him made her feel stupidly weak and miserable.

'I'm sorry,' she muttered as he swung round. 'I stayed in bed longer than usual.'

'I don't know why you don't stay in bed until after I've gone,' he said, striding across the room to pass her on the way to the shower.

'Then I'd never see you,' Elizabeth replied.

145

'If we didn't have breakfast together—'

He glanced at her with cold blue eyes—a look she hated but had come to expect from him. 'That's what I meant,' he said, and shut himself in the bathroom.

Usually, when they encountered each other like this, she would hurry to get dressed and go down to the morning room to wait for him to join her for breakfast. But that morning, though she hastily dressed in jeans and a short-sleeved top, she felt constrained to remain in the bedroom.

Eventually Mike came out, looking startled to find her there. He began to dress hurriedly in his usual business clothes, choosing a patterned blue tie to match his pale blue shirt. Elizabeth watched, not knowing how to break the barriers between them.

'Mike . . .' she ventured, 'we've got to talk.'

'About what?' he asked, combing his hair in front of a long mirror. How tall and fine he was, moving with athletic grace, but shut away from her behind invisible walls.

'Aunt Helen's coming home today.'

'I know that.'

'Yes, but . . . It's going to make a difference.'

'I can't see why,' he said, picking up his jacket and heading for the door. 'Look, I'm in a hurry. I've got an important meeting this morning.'

She went after him, saying plaintively, 'We *never* talk!'

'Of course we do. We discuss the weather, and what Bran's been up to. All very civilised. Small talk over the cornflakes, like most couples.'

He ran lightly down the stairs, leaving Elizabeth to follow more slowly, wearied by the constant battling that was all she now shared with her husband. She had to make him listen somehow.

In the morning room, the usual hot dishes had been laid out, with a pot of coffee, cereals, fruit juice and toast. They sat opposite each other at the small table with sunlight pouring in through an open french window leading to Helen's beloved garden. Bran was out there, sniffing around, but he soon came padding into the room to greet his master and mistress with wagging tail. He went to each of them in turn to be petted and stroked before he lay down in the sunlight, his head on paws.

'So what's troubling you about Helen's homecoming?' Mike asked. 'I thought you were pleased about it.'

'I am. It's just . . . Are you going to go on working so late every day? If you're not here in the evenings, Aunt Helen will get curious.'

'So tell her I'm busy.'

As usual, he had half his mind on his breakfast and the rest on a newspaper lying folded beside his plate. Elizabeth was used to being ignored, but that morning his lack of interest made her want to scream.

'Busy doing what?' she demanded before she could stop herself. 'I know you're not always at the office. There can't possibly be that much work to do. And last night . . . I tried to phone you. There was no answer from the office.'

He glanced across at her. 'Checking up on me, were you?'

'I wanted you to come home early, so that we could talk! You were so anxious to live at Belle Mer, but you're never here to enjoy it. Where do you go? Who do you see?'

'Why, are you jealous?'

The bitter scorn in his voice stung her into jumping up. She walked to the window and stood staring at the garden, her arms tightly folded as if she could hold in her despair. Jealous? Oh, yes, she was. Bitterly, furiously jealous of whatever woman kept him away from her. Or was it women in the plural? She guessed that any woman would do, since he couldn't have Marie-Clair.

'I suppose you haven't thought about the possibility of gossip,' she said hoarsely. 'How long will it be before people are talking about us? Married five weeks and already you're out with other women!'

'I'm very discreet,' he said. 'Don't worry, Helen will never hear that kind of rumour about me. I'm much too careful.'

Elizabeth flung herself round, pain flooding through her. 'You mean you use the bungalow? How can you sit there and calmly admit it? How *can* you, Mike?'

'Our agreement didn't include my turning celibate,' he growled, his eyes glinting with anger. 'I warned you what would happen. If you don't like it, are you prepared to change your mind and be a proper wife?'

She stared at him, her eyes huge and hurt in her pale face, her arms wrapped round herself. 'I . . . I don't know.'

With slow, purposeful movements, he came out of his chair and began to walk around the table towards her, holding her with his eyes. A shiver ran down her spine and she unfolded her arms ready to fend him off.

'Mike . . .' she managed, 'please don't. You frighten me when you look like that.'

Three feet from her, he stopped, an eyebrow tilting sardonically. 'I didn't think you were afraid of anything. You're frightened of *me*? Why? I've never hurt you.'

'You're always hurting me!' The words burst from her and she instantly regretted them because they revealed too much of her real feelings. 'You hurt me the first time we met, remember? I was bruised for days. You're bigger than I am. You always look so angry. You never smile at me, you're never tender. Of course I'm afraid!'

Beside her, Bran was on his feet, disturbed by their raised voices. From her eye corner she saw the dog prick his ears, looking from her to

149

Mike and back again, but her attention was fixed on her husband's taut, beloved face. He was looking at her as if he had never seen her before.

'Tender?' he got out with a curl of his lip. 'God, woman . . .' Whirling away, he swept his jacket from the back of his chair and went to the door, where he paused to look round with hooded eyes and say, 'I'll be home tonight as soon as I can. We can't possibly let Helen guess that we're about as compatible as oil and water, now can we?'

The door slammed behind him—he was always slamming doors, leaving Elizabeth rigid with misery, torn between love and hate.

Bran went softly across the carpet, whining a little as he examined the closed door before turning to pad back to Elizabeth as if he couldn't understand why his master had gone without a word to him. The dog's bewilderment echoed her own and she bent to hug him, closing her eyes against a rush of tears.

'I know how you feel,' she told Bran. 'I love him, too.'

*　　　*　　　*

Promptly at eleven o'clock, Finch the butler announced the arrival of Miss Edith Carrick, the nurse-companion whom Mike had engaged as a temporary measure to ease Helen through the first weeks of her

150

convalescence. Elizabeth had protested that a nurse was not necessary, but her aunt had been in agreement with Mike, as always, saying that it really wasn't fair to expect Elizabeth to do all the nursing.

Elizabeth, however, had so little to do that she would have welcomed the responsibility of looking after her aunt, though that might have caused its own problems with Helen inevitably noticing that she was less than happy. Maybe a nurse was the best answer. With Helen installed in the nursery suite, Elizabeth and Mike could go on with their war in private.

Edith Carrick was a brisk, no-nonsense woman of middle years. She had seen her future domain before, when she came for interview, but now that she was moving in she checked everything again, making sure the rooms were spotless.

'I did warn you I never prepare meals, didn't I?' she said, glancing into the kitchenette. 'Hot drinks I don't mind, but cooking is not part of my function.'

'So you said before,' Elizabeth replied. 'That's perfectly all right. Mrs Finch will cook for us all.'

'So long as we understand each other,' Miss Carrick said crisply. 'Very well, Mrs Delaval. If you'll leave me to settle in I'll be ready to accompany you to the hospital to pick up your aunt. Two o'clock, didn't you say?'

*   *   *

At two o'clock, Elizabeth drove Miss Carrick to the hospital where Helen was waiting fully dressed. Getting her into the back of the car with her leg still in plaster proved an awkward operation, but at last she was comfortably settled and her wheelchair folded in the boot. Then just as Elizabeth was about to climb into the car, hurried footsteps made her look up to see Nathan Frazer arriving, carrying a bunch of flowers.

'I didn't realise you'd be here so early,' he said. 'I almost missed you.' He bent to speak to Helen through the open window, giving her the flowers. 'I'm so glad you're well enough to go home. Take good care of yourself, though.'

Helen smiled at him, saying softly, 'I will. Come and visit us, Nathan, if you're out near Belle Mer.'

'I'll do that,' he said, straightening to look sidelong at Elizabeth as he closed the car door.

By that time, Miss Carrick had installed herself in the passenger seat. Her impatience to be gone was an almost tangible thing.

'Well,' said Nathan with awkward heartiness, 'how's married life?'

'Oh, marvellous,' Elizabeth replied. 'How are *you*?'

'Me? Oh . . .' He shrugged and took a handkerchief from his pocket, making a show of cleaning his glasses. 'I'm fine, thanks. I heard from Gayle. When the business of the will is cleared up, she's giving me first refusal on the car-hire business.'

'That's good,' said Elizabeth. 'If you need an extra receptionist, let me know. I might be glad of something to do.'

Slipping his glasses back on, he looked fully at her for the first time. '*You*?'

'Well, Aunt Helen has a full-time nurse, and we've got staff to look after the house and garden. I keep trying a bit of journalism, but really all I am is a part-time dog-sitter.'

'Dog-sitter?' Nathan queried.

'Yes.' Her mouth stretched in a wry smile. 'Mike has a Great Dane.'

'But . . . would he let you work?' Nathan asked.

'It's hardly a case of his allowing me, Nathan. If I decide I need a job then I'll get a job. Mike won't mind. Don't they say a career makes a woman more interesting to her husband? Sharpens her mind up, and all that?'

Nathan smiled, though his grey eyes remained mournful. 'I would imagine you're quite interesting enough as you are. But I'd better let you go. I'll see you some time.'

* * *

'Oh, it's so lovely to be home!' Helen sighed as she sat in her small sitting room with her plastered leg supported by a stool. 'Just look at

153

that view—that's what I've missed. I really believe Belle Mer has the loveliest views on the island. Ben always said the same.'

'Yes, I know,' Elizabeth replied.

'And now it will be yours, and Mike's. I'm so glad he decided to buy it. I must admit I'll feel more comfortable with him as a landlord rather than Gayle. Just fancy it being his home once. That *was* a coincidence.'

'Yes, wasn't it?' Elizabeth said lightly.

Miss Carrick was fussing around, pushing cushions behind Helen to make her comfortable. 'I really think your aunt would be better in bed, Mrs Delaval,' she chafed. 'The journey must have tired her. It's only when one comes out of hospital that one realises just how weak one still is. We don't want to rush things.'

'Oh, please!' Helen laughed. 'Don't bundle me into bed just yet. I promise I'll sit quietly and behave myself. Come and sit down, Elizabeth. Or have you lots of things to do?'

'Nothing, unfortunately,' Elizabeth replied. 'I mean . . . of course I'm glad to be able to spend sometime with you, but I'm beginning to feel like a spare part.'

They were interrupted by the arrival of Mrs Finch, bringing a tray of tea with a cake which Elizabeth had baked and decorated to welcome Helen home. Behind the housekeeper, Finch carried an enormous florist's box addressed to Mrs Sorensen.

154

'For me?' Helen asked in delight. 'Good heavens, who on earth . . . Miss Carrick, have we a pair of scissors, please? These knots look impossible.'

At last the string parted and the box opened to reveal two huge bouquets of red roses, separately wrapped. Helen gently parted the cellophane which protected the velvety crimson blooms, and took out the card enclosed there. Having read it, she looked up with tears in her eyes, silently handing the card to Elizabeth.

'Welcome home,' it read. 'Mike.'

'You really do have the most thoughtful husband in the world,' Helen said softly. 'I hope you appreciate him. Oh . . . look, these other roses are for you. There's another card, with your name on it.'

The second card read, simply enough, 'For Elizabeth,' and for a split second she actually believed that those two noncommittal words held some message of hope. Then she realised that it was more likely a gesture for her aunt's benefit. Mike had never sent his wife flowers before; such thoughtful ideas only seemed to occur to him where Helen was concerned.

'I've so much to be thankful for,' said Helen, relaxing against her cushions. 'If only Ben . . . But it's no good thinking like that, is it? From now on I'll try to look to the future. I have my home, and you and Mike. And some day my great-nieces and nephews will be running about the place. I've got a lot to look forward to.'

'Yes, you have,' Elizabeth agreed, her voice unsteady. There might be a child about the place sooner than anyone expected—next spring, for instance.

'Why, what's wrong?' asked Helen, ever alert to her niece's moods.

'Nothing,' Elizabeth lied, sinking down beside her to kiss her thin cheek. 'I'm just so glad to have you home at last.'

After a while, it became apparent that Helen was feeling tired, so Miss Carrick had her way and the patient went to bed, pale and worn but obviously contented. That was worth all her own troubles, Elizabeth thought. Her aunt's peace of mind had cost her dear, but now that Helen was home she knew she could have done nothing else. The problem from now on would be keeping Helen in ignorance of the real situation.

On her way downstairs, Elizabeth encountered Finch, who seemed to have been waiting for her.

'Mr Delaval called,' he informed her. 'I told him you were with Mrs Sorensen and he said not to bother you. I'm afraid he's unavoidably detained at the office and will be late for dinner.'

'I see,' said Elizabeth. 'Thank you, Finch.'

As the butler departed kitchenwards, she flung herself into the lounge and ran across to

156

tear the french windows open and step into the garden, fighting back futile tears. Mike had promised to be home. Promised! Who was the 'unavoidable business' this time—blonde, brunette or redhead? How could he keep on doing this so blatantly?

As she ate her lonely dinner with Bran lying disconsolate by her chair, the roses in their crystal vase on the table mocked her. Why had Mike bothered to send them—as a placatory gesture?

Bran sat up, prickling his ears, and with a little 'woof' got to his feet just as Elizabeth, too, heard her husband's voice in the hall. A moment later he appeared, still in his business suit, bending briefly to rub the dog's ears before meeting Elizabeth's eyes.

'I'm sorry,' he said. 'It really was unavoidable. I had to clear some things up before I go to Paris.'

Her head went tight and hot, and all her muscles seemed to clench. 'Paris?'

'Yes. I'm afraid they've called a meeting of the full board. I'm catching the evening flight.'

'Tonight?' She didn't believe her ears.

Looking at her across those meaningless roses, he sat down as Finch came in to lay a place and serve a main course of lamb cutlets. 'I'd ask you to come with me,' Mike said, 'but as Helen's only just come home I assume you'd prefer to stay. Anyway, it's only a flying visit. I should be home in a couple of days.'

Elizabeth said nothing, but she attacked her lamb with unnecessary vigour, her mind filled with pictures of Marie-Clair wrapped in Mike's arms in semi-darkness. Eventually Finch withdrew, leaving a taut silence in the room.

After a while, Mike said. 'I see you got the roses.'

'Yes,' she replied in a brittle voice. 'Aunt Helen was thrilled. She said I had the most thoughtful husband in the world.'

'And you don't agree?'

Not trusting herself to reply, she merely flashed him a furious look, almost exploding with the wild mixture of emotions that filled her—jealousy, anger, despair, misery.

'Look, Elizabeth . . .' he said with a sigh of irritation. 'This problem that's blown up at head office is not my fault.'

'I didn't say it was!'

'No, but you're annoyed with me because of it. I thought you'd be glad to see the back of me for a couple of days. Maybe I should stay away longer—a week? Two?'

'Maybe you plan to, anyway,' she got out.

The silence lengthened until, with his temper barely held, Mike said ominously, 'What's that supposed to mean?'

'Nothing,' Elizabeth muttered. 'Of course you have to go, I'm sorry I said anything.'

'Suddenly you're the possessive wife,' he said derisively. 'Isn't it about time you made up your mind exactly what you do want?' With

158

which he laid knife and fork across his plate and got up.

'You haven't finished your meal!' Elizabeth cried.

'I'm not hungry,' he growled. 'I'm going up to pack. I'll look in and have a word with Helen on the way. Presumably you'll be good enough to drive me to the airport?'

'Yes, of course,' she sighed, her moment of rebellion over. What was the point of arguing with a man impervious as rock? Let him go to Paris. Let him see Marie-Clair. What did Elizabeth care? Except that she did care, stupid though it was. Every bleak look, every bitter word struck painfully at her heart, but every time she tried to get through to Mike she encountered barriers she could never hope to breach. How could she tell him she suspected she was carrying his child?

She let Bran out into the garden to have a run in golden evening light where gulls wheeled and the sea sighed around the distant headland. Part of her wanted to go to Mike, to try again to talk with him, but the rest of her felt too soul-weary to batter hopelessly against those barriers. He seemed to be trying to shut her out of his life entirely now that he had what he wanted; he had Belle Mer, but he wasn't enjoying his victory any more than she was. Their whole life together had become pointless.

'Helen's resting,' he said when he returned

bringing an overnight case. 'Miss Carrick only let me stay for a minute. She's a bit of a dragon, isn't she?'

Elizabeth smiled wryly. 'Efficient, though, and Aunt Helen seems to like her.'

'Helen likes everyone,' said Mike. 'How on earth a woman like her came to be married to Sorensen I'll never figure out.'

'She sees only the good in people.'

He looked her up and down, a corner of his mouth lifting. 'Pity you don't take after her. Well, shall we go?'

The Mercedes waited on the drive and Mike climbed behind the wheel, giving her instructions on handling his car as they travelled beneath a pastel-coloured sky to the airport. He pulled into the car park and got out to remove his case from the boot. Elizabeth, too, left the car, looking round the airport buildings with a breeze playing in her hair and her thoughts bleak.

'Don't bother to see me off,' Mike said from behind her. 'Get back home. And drive carefully. I'd hate my car to be scratched.'

'You never did think I was much of a driver,' she replied, turning to look up at him. 'Remember that first evening we had dinner? That mud on the road . . .' Her voice tailed off as the memory of the evening came back in its entirety and she recalled how it had ended, with her locked in Mike's arms, clinging to him as to a lifeline.

His expression told her he was remembering, too, with cool irony. 'Seems like a long time ago,' he said quietly. 'It might have been two different people. Funny how things change—and all those other clichés.'

'Yes.' She looked down at the tarmac between them, tears tugging behind her eyes. 'Well, you'd better go. Don't miss your flight. Give my regards to everyone.'

'I'll do that.' He bent and set down his case, then stepped forward and caught her in his arms, looking down into her startled face. 'Well, aren't you going to kiss me goodbye?'

Before she could move, his mouth captured hers, harshly at first. But subtly the kiss altered to a sweet, cajoling passion that made emotion swirl through her. Throwing her arms round his neck, she kissed him back, trying to tell him how much she really cared. He responded by holding her tightly, moulding her to the length of his body.

Weeping, she hid her face in his shoulder, clinging to him desperately. 'Come back to me, Mike,' she murmured brokenly. 'Please come back to me.'

'Of course I'll come back,' he replied, his breath warm in her ear. 'I've got to, haven't I? I don't want to upset Helen any more than you do.'

Wincing with pain, she let her arms relax and Mike let her go, a finger tipping up her chin so that he could study her tear-strewn

161

face.

'Funny how you can be nice to me just when I'm leaving,' he said dryly. 'Don't worry, I'll be back. Belle Mer will always bring me back.'

'Belle Mer!' she choked. 'It's always Belle Mer! It's just a house—just bricks and mortar. *Why* is it so important to you?'

'Even if I told you, I doubt if you'd understand,' he said. 'Goodbye, Elizabeth. Take care of Bran for me.'

Through eyes drowned with tears, she watched him walk away until he was lost to view inside the airport buildings. He didn't look back once. All he cared about was his house, and his car, and his dog—and Helen. He didn't care at all for the girl he was slowly tearing apart.

She got behind the wheel of the Mercedes thinking that she would drive it very fast and maybe crash it, and kill herself. *That* would get through to Mike. But such desperate measures were not in her nature. She was too much aware of the harm she might cause, to her aunt and to the tiny scrap of life inside her, which already she loved with a fierce emotion that amazed her. If Mike didn't want her love then she would give it all to her baby—his baby.

She sat in the car for a long time, eventually seeing Mike's plane lift off and head out over the sea, taking him towards Paris, and Marie-Clair.

CHAPTER NINE

The transfer to Belle Mer had tired Helen more than anyone realised—with the exception of Miss Carrick, who seemed grimly pleased to be keeping her patient immobile.

'I did warn you about trying to rush things,' the nurse said to Elizabeth the following morning. 'She ought to have gone straight to bed instead of sitting up having a tea party. It was too much all at once. Now she'll have to take it really easy for a few days.'

Worried, Elizabeth went in to see her aunt, who looked exhausted, with dark circles under her eyes, though she managed to smile and fend off Elizabeth's anxious enquiries.

'I'll be all right—really. They always said it would take time. I was restless in the night— the strange bed, and being here again, without Ben . . . It's difficult, Elizabeth. But you're not to worry about me. In a day or two I'll be fine.'

'I just wish I'd listened to Miss Carrick,' Elizabeth sighed. 'But you seemed so perky.'

'And Miss Carrick is such an old bossy-boots,' Helen smiled. 'But her heart's in the right place. She and I will get along fine. How are you, love? You look a bit off colour yourself. Missing Mike, I suppose. Never mind, he'll be back soon. When your husband's an important man you have to get used to occasional partings.'

After lunch, while her aunt rested, Elizabeth took Bran for a run, going down to the bay, which was swarming with holidaymakers. Dinghies tacked to and fro in a brisk breeze, people swam or sunbathed, and the tables outside the inn were all packed with tourists. Bran seemed to know which way they were going, for he led Elizabeth straight up the lane to the Hardings' rambling old house.

The door was opened by Dave. 'Peggy's not here,' he said. 'Off swimming, I think. Not that that makes any difference, if you'd like to come in. I was in the middle of some paperwork, but I could do with a cup of tea.'

The kitchen and sitting room were in their usual cheerful muddle, the table strewn with accounts books. Dave filled a kettle, splashing himself with water and making Elizabeth think how out of place a huge, bearded, clumsy male could be in a kitchen.

'Angela's still away, then,' she commented. 'You'll have to let me know when she's due back. I'll come and give you a hand to get the place ready for her.'

'That's nice of you,' Dave said glumly, stuffing his hands in the pockets of low-slung jeans. 'You might as well know, Elizabeth . . . she may not be back at all.'

'Oh. I'm sorry.'

He shrugged, giving her a sidelong glance. 'You knew, didn't you?'

'Let's say I was beginning to wonder. Mike hasn't said anything, if that's what you're thinking.'

'No, Mike wouldn't,' Dave replied, leaning against the sink. 'He's too much of a friend. It was all my fault. I . . . made a bit of a fool of myself last summer. Another woman, you know. It was nothing—just a stupid fling. I was flattered that she found me attractive. I took her out sailing and we ended up on a lonely beach and . . . well, you know.'

'It's really none of my business,' Elizabeth said, troubled by such frank confidences.

'Isn't it? You could be wrong there. You haven't asked me who the other woman was.'

'Why, would I know her?'

Dave shrugged again, folding his arms across his chest. 'It was Gayle Sorensen.'

'Oh,' Elizabeth sighed.

'You see,' Dave went on, apparently anxious to unburden himself, 'I felt so bloody guilty I didn't have the sense to keep my mouth shut. After a few months, after Gayle was long gone and the whole thing seemed like a bad dream, I confessed all to Angie. It was a shock for her, but she seemed to understand. Then, earlier this year, she said she needed time to think and space to breathe, so she went off to her parents. It's beginning to look as though she won't come back.'

'Does Peggy know?' she asked.

'She knows we're having problems. She

165

doesn't know exactly why.'

'Dave, I'm so sorry,' she breathed, impulsively laying a hand on his arm. 'I really had no idea. I know Mike was furious with Gayle, but I had no idea it was because of you.'

A wry smile stirred his unkempt beard. 'He told me about that. He mistook you for her, didn't he? I'm only glad it didn't spoil things between you for ever. He always used to say that Angie and I gave him faith that marriage could work. He had his doubts about that, after his own troubles. So I suppose it was a shock to him, too, when the so-called perfect marriage went down the drain. You should have heard him sound off at me! He called me fifty kinds of a damn fool.'

'But really he blamed Gayle,' she commented.

'I'm afraid so. But then he didn't care much for anyone connected with Ben Sorensen, and he was right off women in general.'

As the kettle boiled, Dave reached to switch it off, dumped tea-bags into a pot and filled it up with hot water. 'Hardly the Ritz, but so long as it's wet and warm, eh?'

'It'll be fine.'

Elizabeth watched him get out cups and milk. He filled a dish with water and set it on the floor for Bran, then poured the tea while Elizabeth sat on a kitchen chair wondering if she dared ask Dave about Marie-Clair.

'Mike okay, is he?' he asked, going back to

his stance by the sink.

'He's fine. He . . . er . . . had to go to Paris for a day or two. Some family business meeting.'

'More trouble, you mean,' Dave snorted. 'That lot are for ever calling crisis meetings. That's one reason Mike prefers to stay clear of the Paris end. He saw enough of that when he was learning the ropes. He always preferred the islands. Of course, he was born and raised here—at Belle Mer, as you probably know.'

'Yes, he told me.'

Absentmindedly, he bent to scratch the dog's neck. 'He was livid when he found the place had been leased to Sorensen.'

'Yes, I know,' she murmured. 'He really does love Belle Mer, doesn't he?'

'All he's got left, in a manner of speaking. Memories, you know. Though, after what happened, I did think he might never want to come back.'

'You mean his break-up with Marie-Clair?' Elizabeth asked, hoping that at last she would learn the truth of that affair.

'Well, there was that, too. But that wasn't what . . . Hasn't he told you about his parents?'

'His parents? He's mentioned them, but . . .'

Dave rubbed the back of his neck, looking unhappy. 'Maybe I shouldn't tell you. He doesn't talk about it much. It hurt him a lot.'

'I'd like to know,' she said softly.

'All right, but don't let on it was me who told

167

you. His parents were drowned—both of them on the same day—in a boating accident, off the bay here.'

Elizabeth sat quite still, horrified, thinking how awful that must have been for Mike. She had never realised that such a tragedy lay in his past.

'When was this?' she asked in a hushed voice.

'About five years ago. They were a very close family. Mr and Mrs Delaval were devoted to each other, and Mike being the only child . . . well, they were proud of him. And he thought the world of them. Anyway, old Henri in Paris decided that Mike needed to broaden his experience, so he had him at head office for a while and then sent him abroad to manage their hotels in the West Indies. He was away when the accident happened.'

Elizabeth was too appalled to reply.

'He flew back at once, of course,' Dave told her, 'though there wasn't much he could do. It was a terrible time, waiting for the bodies to be washed up. Half the family came over—and his fiancée, though that didn't seem to help much.'

'Marie-Clair came?' she managed.

Dave nodded, pulling a face. 'She wasn't much of a comfort to him, if you ask me. She was mainly put out because the wedding had to be postponed. Well, of course it did; he could hardly get married just after a tragedy

168

like that. So Marie-Clair flounced off back to Paris and the next I heard about her she was marrying Raoul—in a fit of pique, I suppose. Mike would never talk about it. I hardly saw him after the funeral, and then he went back to Barbados. But he wrote and said he'd be back—back to Belle Mer, to fill it with his own children and make it happy again.'

'Is that what he said?' Elizabeth breathed, a hand unconsciously touching her flat stomach. 'Oh, Dave . . .'

'Here now!' he exclaimed. 'I didn't mean to make you cry. It's all worked out for the best. Don't upset yourself. He's got over it by now.'

He was wrong, she thought. Mike hadn't got over any of it, especially not losing Marie-Clair. Yes, he had Belle Mer, and there would be at least one child. But as for happiness . . .

* * *

Finding her aunt still sleeping, Elizabeth sat on the verandah in a swing seat with the dog beside her. His smooth tawny coat felt warm and comforting to her stroking fingers, but how she wished that Mike was there lying beside her, letting her stroke his hair and his tanned skin, and mocking her the way he used to do. Even his taunts had been preferable to the deep-freeze atmosphere that surrounded him now.

'Excuse me, Mrs Delaval,' Finch's voice

interrupted her yearning thoughts. 'Mr Frazer on the phone for you.' He had brought the instrument with him on a long wire.

Elizabeth lifted the receiver, swallowing to clear a lump from her throat. 'Hello? Nathan?'

'Elizabeth.' He sounded hesitant. 'Hello, how are you? How's your aunt?'

'She's tired, but not too bad,' Elizabeth replied.

'Oh, good. Listen . . . what you said yesterday, about taking a job. Were you serious?'

Had she been serious? She wasn't sure. It was just a thought that had been in the back of her mind for some time. 'Why . . . yes, I think I was. You surely haven't found something for me already?'

'No, not exactly,' Nathan replied. 'Nothing permanent, that is. I didn't like to say anything yesterday. To be honest I was surprised you wanted to work. The fact is, a few days ago my secretary tore a tendon in her leg. She's been told to rest for a couple of weeks. So I'm in a bit of a bind. Most people are already tied up, with the season and everything, and the work's beginning to pile up. I just wondered if you could fill in for me—a couple of hours a day would do, maybe when Helen's resting. Whenever it suits you.'

Unknowingly, he was offering her a brief respite from Belle Mer, where she had begun to feel like a privileged internee. 'Nathan, of course I'll help you out. I'd be delighted.'

170

'What will your husband say?' he asked.

'He's not going to object to my being out for a few hours a day,' she assured him. 'Aunt Helen's well cared for, and the house runs like clockwork. When do you want me to start?'

'Tomorrow?'

'Tomorrow's fine. The afternoon, I think. Say two o'clock?'

'Bless you!' came the reply. 'You're a life-saver!'

Her aunt thought that helping Nathan out was the least she could do after all his kindness, and Elizabeth could see no harm in taking a temporary post with an old and valued friend. That was all Nathan was to her—a friend—he knew it and she knew it. Besides, if Mike could go his own way then so could she. This job would ease her back into office routine and perhaps help her find a more permanent occupation, at least until her baby needed her. She had to have some sort of life of her own, especially now that a happy marriage had been denied her.

*   *   *

At least the small secretary's office at Sorensen Car Hire was a total change from Belle Mer, and the work gave her no time to brood. She seldom even had a chance to glance out of the window at the comings and goings in the airport car park, so absorbed was

171

she in learning the intricacies of booking forms and hire agreements.

In fact, the work kept her so busy that, on her second day at the office, she failed to see the Mercedes arrive, with Finch at the wheel, to pick up Mike on his return from France.

At the end of the afternoon, she returned to Belle Mer as usual. She was crossing the hall, on her way to the stairs to look in on her aunt, when the lounge door was flung open and Mike appeared, stone-faced, dressed in casual shirt and slacks. Her immediate reaction of relief and pleasure was swamped by depression as she read the continued animosity in his eyes.

'You're home,' she said, affecting a laugh that came out breathy and nervous. 'How was the meeting?'

'The meeting was a waste of time, as usual,' he replied, adding heavily, 'And how was *your* day?'

'Busy. I'm doing some secretarial work for Nathan.'

'So I've been informed. It was quite a homecoming—phoning up to ask my wife to meet me, only to be told by the butler that Mrs Delaval has taken a job with her old boy-friend!'

The scorn in his voice flailed across her nerves, making her stiffen. 'I'm sure Finch didn't put it like that. I'm just filling-in while Nathan's secretary's off sick. I never thought

172

for a minute that you'd object.'

'Well, I do,' he said flatly. 'And I don't intend to discuss it in the hall. Go and see your aunt—we'll talk about this later.'

The door closed, leaving her sadly contemplating the prospect of more arguments. Nothing she did ever seemed to be right for Mike. She trailed up the stairs, composing herself and putting on a bright smile for Helen's benefit. Her aunt, seeming refreshed by a couple of days' complete rest, was up and dressed, sitting by her open balcony doors.

Proudly, Helen showed off the silk scarf Mike had brought for her from Paris. 'Isn't he marvellous? Fancy taking the time to think about me. What did he bring you, love?'

'Oh, I've . . . I've hardly had a chance to see him yet. I came straight up to see how you were. You look better.'

'Yes, I feel much better. But you're not to worry about me. I know you'll want to be with Mike this evening. Edith and I are going to play Scrabble, aren't we, Edith?'

The nurse looked up from her knitting. 'Just for a short while. Don't want to overtax you yet.'

Helen laughed. 'With you around, there's no danger of that! Elizabeth, run along and make yourself glamorous for that lovely man of yours. Don't waste your time hovering around me. I intend to get well, and that's exactly what I shall do. Hermione Bessamer called today and invited me to take a cruise with them later in the year, when I've got rid of this plaster. You see, I still have my friends. Your main concern ought to be Mike. So run along, do. And *stop worrying*!'

Elizabeth 'ran along' to the master suite, where she took a quick shower and put on a cool sundress in pink cotton trimmed with lace, a relief after being cooped up in the office all day in sensible skirt and blouse. She brushed her hair until it shone, and spent some time on her make-up. But she went downstairs with her heart like lead.

Bran's barking drew her to the verandah, from where she saw Mike and the dog out in the sunlit garden, running and wrestling as though they were trying to tire each other out. Slowly, Elizabeth walked across the grass towards the pair, and Mike picked himself up, tossing a stick for Bran to race after. As the dog shot away, Mike gave Elizabeth a veiled look.

'You look very nice,' he told her. 'What's all that in aid of? Trying to take my mind off Nathan Frazer?'

'I thought I'd be comfortable,' she replied. 'And don't make out you mind about Nathan. He needed some help and so he turned to me. Is there something wrong with that?'

'It depends why he turned to you in particular. He always had a yen for you. You

174

were the one who didn't want people to gossip about us. Wasn't there someone else he could have asked?'

'Everyone's busy with the tourist season,' Elizabeth explained. 'Besides, I wanted to work. I told him I was thinking of looking for a job.'

'Why?'

'Because I've got nothing useful to do here!'

He glanced at the house. 'Keep your voice down—Helen can probably see us.' Stepping closer, he looped his arms around her waist, giving her a tight smile. 'Better put on a show for her, I suppose. So you decided you'd work, did you? Without even consulting me?'

'I thought this was an open marriage, with both of us doing as we pleased,' she retorted, but she let her hands slide up to his shoulders and linked her fingers behind his neck.

If her aunt was watching, the two of them probably looked like lovers. From that distance Helen couldn't possibly detect the bristling hostility in the air between them, or the sexual charge that made Elizabeth tremble.

'You don't need a job!' Mike gritted through his teeth. 'You've got Helen here, and a house to keep, not to mention a lively dog. I won't have my wife working, especially for Nathan Frazer. If you want something to do, you can join one of the voluntary associations.'

'I might do that, as well as having a career,'

175

she shot back.

'Why do you need a career? You certainly don't need the money.'

'That's your money, not mine. I want to support myself. I want independence.'

An angry breath escaped him as his arms tightened, pulling her full against him. 'You've got your independence. I'm giving you an allowance, aren't I? Though I notice you're hardly touching it. Still determined not to take anything from me, are you? For God's sake, I'm your husband!'

'Which doesn't make you my lord and master!' she snapped back, wishing he would let her go. She had almost forgotten the way he could make her feel, his physical nearness swamping all her senses with the feel of his body against hers, his hair thick and silky to her fingers, the clean scent of him assailing her. Looking into his eyes, she saw that he was equally aware of her.

'Doesn't it?' he said in an odd, gruff voice. His fingers stroked her bare shoulder and trailed softly up her throat to loop her hair behind her ear. He laid his hand on her cheek, lashes veiling his blue eyes as he watched her mouth for a second. Her lips softened as he bent and kissed her briefly, gently, making her tremble. His lips clung sweetly to hers as he lifted his head—and then she saw the derision in his eyes.

'You'll do anything for your aunt's sake,' he

176

taunted. 'Even tremble in my arms as though you like being near me. What will you do when she's well, and with us frequently?'

'Will you ever be at home?' she responded raggedly. 'I thought you preferred to avoid me.'

'I do! And you know why, don't you?'

His mouth closed over hers again, punishingly brutal this time as he held her plastered to his body, one hard arm across her waist, the other hand spread in her hair. Elizabeth responded in kind, locking her arms round his neck while her mouth answered the feverish demands of his. Despair and fury warred inside her, love and hate fusing in a wild mixture that made her want to hurt him as he hurt her. But she could feel herself losing the battle, wilting under his onslaught to her senses.

Abruptly, he let her go, his hands on her shoulders thrusting her away as he glared at her with eyes that blazed blue fire. His chest heaved as he drew a deep, shuddering breath, and said hoarsely, 'You know how to torment me, don't you? God, and I thought you were different! You had it all planned. Oh, yes, you'd go along with me—for Helen's sake. But you're determined not to let me have any joy of it, aren't you? All I ever wanted was Belle Mer and now, slowly and surely, you're poisoning it for me.'

'I didn't plan it! How can you say that?

Mike—'

'Hush!' He pulled her close again, an arm clamped round her shoulders as he turned her towards the house. He held her fiercely, his fingers pressing into the flesh of her upper arm, his head bent to hide her face from anyone watching from the house. His smile looked more wolfish than pleasant as he said, 'Don't let Helen think we're having a row.'

'Oh, Mike,' she whispered brokenly, resting her weary head on his shoulder. 'We ought to have known it wouldn't work. I don't think I can take much more, even for Aunt Helen's sake.'

'I don't think either of us has much choice,' he muttered.

The house towered over them now. If her aunt had been watching, which somehow Elizabeth doubted, then they had gone from her sight by now. Feeling wretched, she eased away from Mike and trailed ahead of him into the lounge.

'Just wait a while, will you?' she sighed, sinking into a settee. 'When my aunt's fit enough to take it, I'll find some way of telling her a version of the truth. No doubt we'll be able to afford a house somewhere. I know you'll want to stay here. I . . . I heard what happened to your parents.'

'Where did you hear it?' he demanded in an oddly strangled voice.

She looked up at him, seeing him withdrawn

behind those shutters she hated. 'Did you think you could keep it a secret for ever? Why didn't you tell me yourself?'

'I'm not going to beg for your pity, if that's what you want,' he growled. 'And you're not to tell Helen anything, ever. I've heard her talk about Sorensen. She thinks he was perfect. A "version" of the truth wouldn't satisfy her; she'd want to know it all. She'd find out that her husband left her hardly anything—not even a secure roof over her head. If *you* can do that to her, I can't.'

'You really care about Helen, don't you?' Elizabeth said, shaking her head. 'You pretend you have no soft feelings, but it's all an act. I wish . . .' She was going to say 'I wish you cared about me,' but she was interrupted by the arrival of Finch, who announced that dinner was served. The moment was lost. Anyway, Mike could never care about her; the only woman he wanted was Marie-Clair.

They slipped, with awful ease, back into the old familiar distant politeness as they ate dinner. Nothing was ever going to change, Elizabeth thought sadly. They were both doomed to live this way for ever, acting out a charade which brought joy to neither of them. They must both have been mad ever to embark on this marriage.

'Something funny?' Mike demanded as her mouth curved in a wry smile.

She glanced across at him, surprised that he

179

had been watching her. 'I was just thinking—you said we were fated for each other. you forgot to mention that it was a malign fate, not a friendly one.'

He said nothing, only watched her with eyes as revealing as blue lakes.

'You haven't said much about your Paris trip,' she added. 'Did you see all the family? How's Paul?'

'Just as much of a little pest as ever,' said Mike with disgust.

'Don't you like children?'

'Not particularly—not when they're left to run wild. Not that it's his fault, poor little devil—any of it.'

Feeling a stillness inside her, as if she were on the verge of an important discovery, Elizabeth breathed, 'Any of what?'

'Nothing,' he said, his mouth shutting like a trap on the word. 'Anyway, why are you so interested in Paul?'

'Because I feel sorry for him. I assume you saw Marie-Clair, too?' She tried to keep her voice casual, but some acid nuance must have been evident, for she saw Mike's lips tighten.

'I did. So what? Just what are you accusing me of, Elizabeth—having an affair with my cousin's wife?'

'I don't know what there is between you!' Elizabeth exclaimed. 'I only know she's on your mind the whole time. You only married me because you couldn't have her.'

He watched her steadily with an expression that said he had no intention of either confirming or denying this charge. 'Did I?'

'Of course you did! You were engaged to her. There was some misunderstanding, and she went off and married Raoul in a fit of pique. And now she's regretting it, she wants you back—and you still want her, I know you do. You're in love with her.'

For a moment he continued to regard her without a flicker of emotion. 'Is that your considered opinion?' he asked. 'You're a rotten psychologist, Elizabeth.' Unhurriedly, he rose from his chair and gave her a smile that had about as much warmth in it as an Arctic winter. 'I'm going to the office to make sure nothing important's come up in my absence. Don't wait up for me, I'll probably be late.'

Elizabeth laid her head in her hands, her eyes aching with unshed tears. 'We can't go on like this. We really can't.'

'Well, it was you who decided it had to be this way,' Mike reminded her coolly, and strode from the room without a backward glance.

*   *   *

She lay awake far into the night waiting for him to come home, but eventually she fell into a dream-haunted sleep full of horrors. When she woke to morning light she felt terrible, but her first thought was for Mike and she looked across at the other bed, seeing it neat and unused. Mike had not been home.

Feeling sick, she lay with an arm across her eyes. Her thoughts roamed incoherently, bringing her nothing but distress. She remembered him saying, 'I thought you were different.' Different from what? Oh, if only he would *talk* to her!

When the bedroom door opened she lay still, watching from beneath her arm as Mike, surprisingly dressed in swimming trunks and damp from the pool, went into the bathroom and turned on the shower. Elizabeth sat up, feeling sluggish, her stomach unsettled. The other bed had not been slept in, of that she was sure. Why had he bothered to come back at all?

Unable to face getting up, she slid back between the sheets shivering a little, curled up into a ball of misery. She heard Mike emerge from the bathroom and begin to dress.

'I know you're awake,' he said eventually.

'I'm not feeling very well,' she muttered.

'So I breakfast alone, do I?'

Stung, Elizabeth wrenched herself to a sitting position, which made her insides churn and her head ache. 'I thought that's how you wanted it! O-oh!' With a groan, she laid a hand to her head, aware of him crossing the room towards her.

A finger under her chin made her look up at him as he frowned. 'You do look a bit pale. Better stay in bed for a while. If you don't feel better soon, I should call a doctor. Not feverish, are you?'

As his hand came on her forehead, she flinched away, only to hear him exclaim in anger as he grabbed her shoulders and sat down next to her, half shaking her.

'Don't do that!' he growled. 'Don't recoil from me. Aren't I allowed to be concerned about you?'

'If you were concerned about me, you wouldn't stay out all night!' she replied bitterly.

'Oh, for God's sake!' He stood up, going to jerk his jacket from its hanger. 'I'm begining to think it would be better if I stayed away permanently.'

'Mike!' she cried, but he was gone, leaving only the echo of the slamming door.

Elizabeth forced her stiff legs out of bed, reeling across the room to grab her wrap and fling it on. A few deep breaths helped to steady her head, but she still felt nauseous as she stumbled down the stairs and made for the morning room—which was empty. Mike had gone without his breakfast.

The smell of the food made her feel even worse, but then Bran came cheerfully wagging up and she bent to put her arms round him and hug him, her eyes full of tears. The dog quivered with pleasure, trying to lick her face until she straightened out of his reach and stared blindly out at the rain drifting across the patio.

'He'll come back,' she whispered to Bran. 'Of course he'll come back. He didn't mean it. Did he?'

CHAPTER TEN

The rain continued to fall, adding to Elizabeth's depression, though a piece of toast and a cup of coffee soon made her feel physically better. There would be no need to call a doctor since she knew exactly what was ailing her. Sooner or later everyone else would know it, too; a woman could not keep that sort of secret for very long.

She spent the morning with her aunt, planning the new décor which Helen wanted for her rooms. She saw herself living in the suite even after she was well, easily available but not interfering with Elizabeth's life.

'Now that Mike's buying the house and taking over all the expenses,' she said, 'really I shall be quite comfortably off. I want to pay my way, not feel a burden. You've given me more than I dared hope for. If I can have a small corner in your lives I'll be perfectly content.'

'You've got a life of your own, too,' said Elizabeth. 'You're not old, Aunt Helen.'

'No. But don't rush me, love.'

Elizabeth's one remaining fear was that Gayle might write, or arrive unexpectedly, and tell Helen that the house had belonged to Mike all the time. But she hoped Gayle was much too self-centred to care what her stepmother was doing. If only Elizabeth could make peace with Mike, everything would be wonderful.

However, that peace remained a wish, though as Elizabeth drove to the car-hire office at the airport through a light drizzle she had the distinct feeling that her aunt knew something was wrong. Helen hadn't said anything, but she had questions in her eyes all the time. One way or another, something would have to be done.

The office seemed to be extra busy that afternoon, with many phone queries to answer and a whole pile of urgent letters which Nathan said must go off before the weekend. After a while, one of the junior receptionists brought Elizabeth a cup of coffee and with relief she switched off the typewriter to take a five-minute break. She turned her chair to look out over the cars in the car park, where a weak sun was just beginning to break through the clouds. Her heart lurched painfully as she glimpsed a familiar figure.

Mike had parked the Mercedes in a far

corner of the car park, as far from Elizabeth's office as was possible. But it was not so far that his tall figure was mistakable, nor the fact that he had his arm round a slim young woman with dark hair.

Stricken, Elizabeth watched as he solicitously saw the woman into the passenger seat and put her suitcase in the boot of the car before himself getting behind the wheel. Sunlight glinted off the pale blue paintwork as the vehicle slid out of the park and away.

Marie-Clair had come to Jersey. It had to be Marie-Clair. Who else would Mike be so tender with?

The office door opened and Nathan said, 'Elizabeth, I . . . Oh!'

Like one in a dream, or a nightmare, she turned her ghost-pale face to look at him. 'Yes?'

He was watching her with a sympathy she found intolerable. 'You saw them, then? I was hoping to distract you. But she could be anyone—an old friend, a relative.'

His cousin's wife, for instance, she thought. 'Yes, I expect that's it,' she replied in a hollow tone. 'Mike will tell me about it tonight. Did you want something?'

'I hoped . . .' He paused and gave her a regretful look. 'I hoped to prevent you from looking out of the window at that precise moment.'

'Why?'

'Well, because . . . It's none of my business. I know, but I was over in the main terminal and I saw them meet. I thought perhaps she was a friend coming to stay at Belle Mer, but from the way they . . .'

She seemed to be protected by a cocoon of shock that prevented her from feeling anything. 'The way they what, Nathan?'

'The way they greeted each other,' Nathan said unhappily. 'She rushed straight into his arms. They . . . they kissed each other, right there in the open. Elizabeth . . . I'm sorry. I really didn't want you to know.'

Turning away, she looked again at the car park, her arms wrapped tightly round her body as if by that means she could stop herself from coming apart.

'Do you know her?' Nathan asked.

She shook her head, swallowing convulsively. 'I'm not sure.'

But she was sure—horribly, sickeningly sure. Mike had been to Paris. He had arranged this with Marie-Clair. He had lied to Elizabeth. Was it to be just a brief visit, a stolen weekend, or was this the way it would all end—Marie-Clair leaving Raoul, Mike leaving Elizabeth?

'I warned you about him,' Nathan said passionately. 'Why didn't you listen to me? Elizabeth, I know you're not happy. Why did you marry him?'

She turned then, not caring if he saw her

187

tears. 'Because I love him,' she said desolately. 'I love him, Nathan.'

*   *   *

That evening she sat alone, with Bran on the carpet at her feet. Mike had not come home for dinner and she had a feeling he would not be home to sleep, either. That morning he had, in his own way, been trying to prepare her for this when he talked about staying away permanently. He had tried to put the blame on her.

If he really wanted Marie-Clair, nothing Elizabeth could do would change his mind. Marie-Clair had always been between them, absent but omnipresent, holding the key to Mike's heart and preventing him from loving anyone else. No doubt she had hurt him in the past, but she possessed the only salve that could soothe those hurts.

But could she make him happy, in the long run? Elizabeth remembered sensing a coldness in Marie-Clair, for all her beauty; young Peggy hadn't liked Mike's former fiancée, and neither had Dave. And it was true that Marie-Clair had abandoned Mike when he needed her most: she had gone off and married Raoul.

Quite suddenly, Elizabeth knew that she couldn't let Mike go, not without a fight. Loving him, she wanted him to be happy, but she doubted if his happiness lay with Marie-

Clair. She had to do something, for her baby's sake, for her aunt's sake, for her own sake. Up to now she had stood back and let him go his own way, but the time had come for her to assert herself.

She stood up suddenly, startling Bran. A new determination fired her blood where before she had been too dejected to fight. If she had to sink her pride and confess her true feelings then she would do it. She would tell Mike about the baby and beg him to reconsider a life with her.

Going up to the master suite, she showered swiftly and dressed in a blouse and skirt of filmy material, white with a pattern of leaves. The blouse had a low neckline and the light fabric was almost see-through, seductive and feminine; but tonight was a time for using all the weapons she possessed. She groomed herself carefully, and added generous sprays of a heady perfume, then stared at her reflection in the mirror.

Mike was not immune to her, that much she knew. If he had to make a choice, which woman would he choose? The wife he desired, who loved him, who was carrying his child; or the woman who had once let him down, who was married to his cousin and had a child of her own?

By the time she got into the car, the sky was almost dark. A last streak of red faded in the west and the evening star began to sparkle.

Fuelled by a burning passion to succeed at any cost, Elizabeth drove through shadowed lanes to the white gates of the bungalow. As she had expected, Mike's Mercedes stood on the drive.

Leaving her car on the verge outside the gate, she walked up the curving drive, feeling tension build inside her at the vision of Marie-Clair with Mike. How would they react to her sudden appearance? Would they try to lie their way out of it, or would they confess their mutual love and ask her to release Mike?

Avoiding the front door, she went through the archway into the courtyard where clematis now dripped scarlet and purple blooms in the light from the lamp beside the door. All the curtains in the house were drawn, with light showing from the main room. The back door—as she discovered when she gently tested it—was unlocked.

Through the open door of the main room came the peaceful strains of a piano concerto, masking any sound Elizabeth might have made. She heard no voices, but through the reeded glass of the door she made out a figure on the settee.

Stretching out a hand, she pushed the door further, seeing soft yellow lamplight on familiar hangings and shining wood. Mike appeared to be alone, the coffee-table covered with paperwork over which he sat in shirt-sleeves, head in hands. There was no sign of Marie-Clair.

As Elizabeth stepped inside the room, her husband looked up, startlement failing to mask the weariness in his heavy-eyed face. He looks miserable, Elizabeth thought with a stab of sympathy. Had he and Marie-Clair quarrelled already?

'Where is she?' she asked.

Mike was staring at her as if she were a ghost. He shot to his feet, sending papers slithering to the floor. 'Elizabeth! What—?'

'Where *is* she?' she said again.

'Where's who?' He seemed not to understand her. 'Who do you mean?'

'You know who I mean!' she cried, clenching her hands fiercely. 'Please don't lie to me any more, Mike. I know Marie-Clair is here.'

'Marie-Clair?' he echoed in apparent bewilderment.

She flung a hand to her head, taking a deep breath in an effort to stay calm. 'Please, Mike, let's talk about this calmly. Don't treat me as though I'm a stupid infant.'

For a moment he stared at her in silence, looking as though he didn't believe his senses. 'What makes you think Marie-Clair is here?'

'I saw you! At the airport. Nathan saw you, too—the way she rushed into your arms when you met her off the plane. I saw you in the car park. You had your arm round her!'

She saw understanding hit him, and then all his shutters came down again, leaving his eyes

191

glinting blue in a face like a mask. 'I see,' he said.

'You're not going to deny it, then?'

'Would it do me any good?' he returned. 'If you saw us, that's proof, isn't it?'

'Then she's here?'

He watched her enigmatically, spreading his hands to encompass the room. 'Take a look for yourself. Well, go ahead, don't just stand there.'

'She's not here, is she?' Elizabeth said flatly.

'Oh, please! Don't take my word for it. Come and take a look.' He strode across the room to grab her wrist and dragged her into the further hall, opening doors, switching on lights. There were two bedrooms and a bathroom, all neat and apparently unused.

'Guest rooms,' Mike said tightly. 'But presumably you'd expect to find my mistress in my bed.'

He all but flung her into a large bedroom like a cosy cave, dark brown walls and ceiling with the covers in the double bed turned back to reveal brown sheets. A shirt was slung over a chair, and only male toiletries stood on the dressing table. From the adjoining bathroom came a damp warmth and a strong scent of Mike's talc and aftershave. Obviously he had recently had a bath.

Laying hold of her again, he took her back to the main room where he nodded at the rear hall. 'You've missed the kitchen and the dining room.'

She moved away from him, aware that she had made a mistake. Obviously Marie-Clair was not at the bungalow. What point was there in searching further and making a complete idiot of herself?

'So where is she?' she asked dully. 'At a hotel?'

'Do you really expect me to tell you?'

Taking a deep breath, she turned to face him, distressed beyond bearing. 'Please tell me the truth, Mike! I know you think you're in love with her, but are you really? She's a married woman. She has a child. What about Raoul and Paul? Have you considered what you're doing to them? You can't be intending to—'

'Don't!' he cut her off sharply. 'Don't say any more. But thank you, Elizabeth. Thank you for your real opinion of me. You want the truth, you shall have it. I did meet a lady at the airport. Yes, she ran and hugged me. And I did have my arm round her—because she was upset.'

'Upset?' she got out. 'About what?'

With eyes as cold as glaciers, he said flatly, 'She wasn't sure what sort of reception she was going to get from her husband. But she needn't have worried—Dave was delighted to see her.'

Elizabeth felt her stomach lurch with shock. For a moment she feared she might be sick.

'Dave? Dave Harding?'

'The lady,' Mike said in a hard tone, 'was Angela Harding.'

Shock made her feel chilled. She stood shivering, mortified and despairing.

'If you'd asked,' he added, 'I'd have told you who she was. I've been in contact with her for some time, trying to arrange a reconciliation between her and Dave. Now, finally, she's decided to come back, but she wanted me there to smooth things over, just in case. As it turned out, it wasn't necessary. I didn't stay very long.'

She croaked. 'Oh . . . Mike!' Tears burst from her and she flung her hands to her face, swaying where she stood, sobbing, 'Oh, Mike. Mike!'

'Is that meant to be an apology?' he asked scathingly.

'Don't be like that,' she begged. 'Please don't be like that. If you knew what I've been thinking . . . I'm sorry. Please forgive me. I thought I was losing you.'

'That ought to have made you very happy,' came the cool reply.

She flung up her head, seeing him blurred through boiling tears. 'It wouldn't. You know it wouldn't!'

'I don't know anything of the sort. You hate me, you said. I make you feel ill. Every time I touch you, you feel soiled. You won't let me give you anything—you wouldn't accept a decent ring. On our wedding night you made me feel like a louse for giving you diamonds, and when I send you roses all I get is sarcasm. If you didn't want to lose me, Elizabeth, you've been going about it in a very peculiar way.'

It was true. All of it was true!

Suddenly she couldn't bear being with him any more. She spun round and fled from the room, through the open back door and across the courtyard. Beneath the archway, a hard hand fell on her arm and she was swung round bodily, to collide with Mike with a force that robbed her of breath. She struggled desperately, but he held her wrists imprisoned.

'Don't be a fool!' he growled at her. 'D'you think I'd let you drive in this state? What would Helen do if something happened to you?'

'Helen?' That struck her as incredibly, hurtingly funny. Hysterical laughter bubbled up inside her. 'You know, you married the wrong woman—you should have proposed to Helen, not me!'

Her head snapped back as he jerked her to him, his arm cruelly tight around her waist. In the lamplight his face was all angles and planes, with eyes that snapped fury at her. 'That isn't very funny!'

'I know.' A shudder ran through her as her laughter died and with a sob she leaned on him helplessly. 'Oh, Mike, it's got nothing to do with Helen. It's us. I'm so unhappy. I love you so much and I can't bear it. All we do is make each other miserable. Why does it have to be that way? Why?'

Close to her ear, he whispered hoarsely, 'What did you say?'

'I said I love you,' she choked, pressing her face to his shirt, where she breathed in the clean scent of him and felt the swift thud of his heart. 'If you'll come back to me, I'll do anything you want. I know it's all been my fault and—'

'Just shut up,' he muttered, his mouth seeking hers with an urgency that made her surge up to meet his kiss on a tidal wave of emotion. The great outpouring of long-denied love swept her up and made her cling tightly to him, their mouths fused in mutual need. Hope made her press closer to him until she felt his body must leave an indelible imprint on her flesh. Maybe he didn't love her, but in time he might learn to care for her, just a little. That was all she asked.

After endless moments she sank exhausted to lean on his chest, her eyes closed against a rush of tears that did not seem to stop. The tidal wave had tossed her up and left her limp as seaweed, wanting only to stay in Mike's arms and rest.

'You're tired out,' he said softly. 'Here, put your arms round my neck.'

The world seemed to gyrate as he lifted her in strong arms that conveyed her with ease beneath the trellis where leaves trembled and stars danced. She felt him kick the back door shut, and then golden lamplight surrounded them as he laid her gently on the settee. His tenderness amazed her as much as the expression of concern on his face.

'I'm sorry about the hysterics,' she murmured wryly. 'I meant to be so calm, and here I am acting like a harridan, or some wilting Victorian female. I can't think what's the matter with me.'

'Can't you? Well, whatever it is, I wish it would happen more often. The wilting bit, I mean. I can only take so much of the bloody-minded, independent, liberated lady. It was fun at first, but lately it's been hell to live with.'

Elizabeth blinked up at him, faltering, 'I . . . don't understand.'

Mike pulled a rueful face, settling himself more comfortably on the floor beside her, his fingers tracing the contours of her cheek. 'I'm just as tired of it as you are. Isn't it time we stopped trying to hack each other to pieces? I'll try if you will.'

'Will you?' She felt bewildered, lightheaded. 'Will you come home to me every night instead of . . .'

'Instead of bringing my work here, all on my own, listening to records, and wondering what the hell I can do to make you forget I blackmailed you into marrying me?'

Dazed, she glanced round the room, where

all the evidence pointed to the truth of his assertion. 'Is this where you've been all those evenings? Here? Alone?'

'I couldn't come home,' Mike said quietly. 'Being near you is too much like torture. I had to stay away, and where else have I got to go but here? So many times I went back to Belle Mer wanting to ask you to forgive me, but either the words wouldn't come, or the time wasn't right. It made me feel vicious, so I kept taking it out on you because I was hurting. It hasn't all been your fault. I was to blame, too. I kept losing my temper when what I really wanted . . .' A fingertip softly brushed the curve of her lips. His gaze followed the movement and he bent slowly, tentatively, to let his mouth caress hers with infinite longing. He looked down at her, his eyes bright and sorrowful. 'If you only knew how much I love you!'

Something jolted inside her, a painful twisting in the region of her heart as she stared at him with eyes that threatened to eclipse her pale face.

'Don't you believe me?' he asked anxiously.

'I just . . . I was so sure that . . . Oh, Mike, hold me! She threw her arms round his neck and felt him draw her to him, holding her as if she were very precious to him.

'Don't cry,' he pleaded. 'Please don't let me make you cry any more. It's over, Elizabeth.' Lifting his head, he bathed her face in kisses, drying her tears with his lips. 'Darling Elizabeth,' he said under his breath. 'Darling, darling Elizabeth.'

'You should have told me,' she wept. 'Why did you let me go on thinking those awful things?'

'To punish you, I suppose.'

'And there weren't any other women? None at all?'

'Only you,' he vowed, and kissed her mouth in a way that made her feel she was drowning. Time stopped as she let herself be drawn into sweet communion with him, her heart wanting to burst with joy.

At length he pulled a little away, settling her more comfortably against the cushions, his eyes dark blue and glowing as he watched her. 'Anyway,' he said with a hint of his old mockery, 'whatever gave you the idea I was a womaniser? I'm no saint, but women have never been one of my weaknesses.'

'I don't know,' she sighed. 'I suppose it was because Nathan said—'

His finger on her lips stopped the words. 'Good old Nathan Frazer, eh? He's been the fly in our ointment right from the start. First he phones me to warn me off, then he tells you I'm a lecher. And what do you suppose was his reason for giving you a job?'

'He needed help.'

'Oh, yes? Or did he want to make trouble between us? You did say he was the one who

199

saw me meet Angela today—and then he made sure you knew all about it, probably suitably exaggerated.'

'But he didn't mean . . .' she began, and stopped herself, wondering if she had been naïve to believe in Nathan's good intentions.

'I suppose I ought to be grateful to him,' Mike murmured silkily. 'After all, if he hadn't put his spoke in you might not have come rushing here tonight, all beautiful and smelling like heaven. Who knows how long we might have gone on fighting?'

Troubled, she rubbed the edge of his shirt neck between her thumb and finger. 'There's still Marie-Clair. How *do* you feel about her, Mike?'

'Lucky,' he said at once. 'Lucky to have escaped a fate worse than death.'

She could hardly believe her ears. 'But you loved her once. You must have done.'

'And you must have been listening to gossip! Where did you get the idea . . . Darling girl.' He stroked her face, pushing her hair behind her ear. 'Maybe I did love her once. Not the way I love you, though, warts and all. Marie-Clair was my virgin goddess, so pure I hardly dared touch her. I worshipped what I thought she was rather than the girl herself.'

'So what happened?'

Smiling, he bent to touch his lips to a corner of her mouth before turning to lean with his back against the settee, holding her hand at his chest. Head resting on her thigh, he looked at the ceiling and sighed heavily.

'I was in Barbados—dispatched there by my grandfather to cure me, I suspect, of my infatuation with Marie-Clair. Unfortunately, distance only lent enchantment. She remained the perfect woman in my mind.' Turning his head to look at her, he grimaced. 'She wasn't perfect, of course, far from it. All the time she was writing love-letters to me she was also fooling around with Raoul. When I came back—when my parents were drowned—she came to Belle Mer and tried her damnedest to seduce me, at just the wrong time. My parents were all I could think about, and all she talked about was the wedding and how soon it could take place. We quarrelled about it and she flew straight back to Paris and married Raoul.'

'Just to spite you?'

'I thought so, at the time. It was a while before I realised why she'd been so anxious to get married, or at least to get me into bed.'

'She was pregnant with Paul?' Elizabeth asked in disbelief. 'You mean, she would have landed you with another man's child?'

'She might have done, if I'd been fool enough to believe her.'

'But she said she loved you!' she said faintly.

'Marie-Clair never loved anyone but Marie-Clair,' he replied, and squinted up at her. '*When* did she say that? To you? In Paris?'

'No, I . . . I saw you with her, in the hall. I

201

couldn't hear most of what you were saying, but I did hear her say she loved you, and then . . . you kissed her.'

In a whirl of motion, Mike stood up, towering over her. 'For God's sake! Is that what made you . . . Why didn't you *tell* me?'

'Because I thought you'd lie to me,' she replied in a small voice.

'Oh, thanks!'

She sat up, reaching out to him. 'Don't be angry, please. I heard her, Mike. I saw you. Maybe I misunderstood what was really going on. You were talking in French.'

'Were we? Oh, hell, darling . . .' He dropped back beside her, holding her hand tightly. 'Why didn't you eavesdrop a little longer? You might have heard me tell her just what I thought of her. You might have seen her try to scratch my eyes out. Yes, I kissed her—enough to let her think she'd won before I gave her the sharp edge of my tongue. She's married to my cousin, whether she likes it or not, and she's got a child to consider. And *I* had a brand new wife with whom I was rapidly falling in love.'

'You were?' she said incredulously. 'Well, you could have fooled me!'

A corner of his mouth lifted in a wry smile as he laid an arm around her and drew her to lean against him. 'I was fooling myself, too. After the fiasco with Marie-Clair, all mixed up with losing my parents at the same time, I swore I'd never care about anyone again. It just wasn't worth the agony. It took me a long time, until after I met you, to realise that a person can't just decide not to fall in love. It happens, whether you want it to or not. This last month or so, I've had plenty of time to think about my own motives concerning you.'

'And?'

'And I think I fell for you that first time on the beach—when you nearly drowned yourself for fear of harmless old Bran. There was something about you, even before I knew who you were. Chemistry I suppose. But your being connected to Ben Sorensen did complicate matters.'

'Just a little,' she murmured drily.

'A mere fraction,' he replied with a heavy sigh. 'Oh, God . . . I was angry with Sorensen, I was attracted to you, I was sorry for Helen, and I wanted Belle Mer. It wasn't all black and white. Marrying you seemed to be the best answer. You were a pretty tough lady, so I thought. I imagined we'd spar all day and make it up in bed every night. But the more I got to know you, the deeper I got my feelings involved. I did *try* to be tender, Elizabeth, but you didn't make it easy for me. Do you know how it feels to be told by someone you love that you make her physically ill just by going near her?'

Hurting for the pain she had caused him, she rubbed her cheek on his shoulder. 'I'm sorry, Mike—I'm sorry for everything. I was all mixed up, too. Jealous, and afraid—and terrified you might guess how I felt and laugh at me. I had to make you keep your distance. You did make me feel ill—with sheer excitement.'

He turned to her, hands on her shoulders as he leaned over her with hope in his eyes. 'Then at the *auberge*, when I made love to you . . . you didn't abhor every second of it?'

'Mike . . .' She touched his dear face and let her hand slip under the open neck of his shirt to adore the feel of his skin. 'If only you'd told me then that you loved me, it would have been wonderful. I felt desolate. I needed you. And you just turned over and went to sleep, as if it had meant nothing.'

'Nothing? It meant everything! But I was tired. I hardly got any sleep the previous night. While you were lying spark out with Tante Véronique's wine, I was sitting up watching you, wondering what I'd done. I had no idea you'd seen me with Marie-Claire. How could I know that? I didn't get into bed until dawn, and then I only slept for an hour or so. Naturally I was shattered the next night, after driving and more fighting with you, and then, finally, reaching some sort of understanding— that's what I thought. I was crazy happy the next morning—until you made me feel like a vile seducer.'

'You should have said!' she cried.

'So should you!' he returned. 'And in future

you will, Mrs Delaval. You'll tell me everything. We'll stop using each other for sniping practice and start communicating. Yes?'

'Yes!' Elizabeth breathed, drowning in blue eyes alight with love.

Mike took her in his arms, kissing her with sweet passion, his mouth moving and enticing until she thought she must melt with delight. She was lost. She was found. She clung to him as he eased her to her feet and stood with his arms circling her, looking into her face with burning eyes.

'How are you feeling?' he asked gruffly.

'Me?' Elizabeth said dreamily. 'Oh, wonderful! What about you?'

'I feel great, but it wasn't me who nearly collapsed a short while ago,' he reminded her, frowning a little. 'And this morning you looked awful. You're not ill, are you?'

'No!' It came out breathy with amusement that faded as she realised she must tell him the truth. 'Not ill, exactly. Mike . . . did you tell Dave that you intended to fill Belle Mer with children?'

'I may have done. Why, what . . .' His face changed. As he interpreted the clues, shock and then dawning wonder wiped away his frown. 'You're not?' he said. 'Are you?'

'I think so. That night at the *auberge*, remember? Do you mind?'

'Mind? Darling girl . . .' Robbed of words,

205

he kissed her, fiercely and tenderly, and bent to lift her up into his arms where he held her close. 'You shouldn't be on your feet. Oh, lord, if I'd known I'd never have let you get so upset. You've got to take care of yourself.'

Laughter bubbled out of her. 'Playing the expectant father already?'

'But of course.' He carried her into the dim-lit hall and through to his bedroom. 'You ought to be in bed. We both ought to be in bed. After a shock like that . . .' As he laid her gently down, his amusement faded, replaced by an immense tenderness that warmed her all through. 'Will you stay with me tonight? I'll phone Finch and let him know. Let's be on our own for once. All on our own.'

'That sounds like heaven,' Elizabeth replied softly.

Mike switched on the bedside lamp, leaned to kiss her again and said, 'I won't be long. Don't go away.'

She had no intention of going anywhere, but when he had gone she got up and undressed completely before climbing between the cool brown sheets. Mike's bed, she thought. Mike's bungalow. It was like having a secret love-nest, deliciously sinful. Thank goodness they were married!

Returning to find her cosily curled in his bed, Mike smiled to himself and went to open a drawer, taking out a box which he presented to her. It was a flagon of perfume from an exclusive salon in Paris. 'I brought you this from my business trip. I forgot to give it to you.'

'You mean I was so rotten to you that you didn't feel like giving me anything,' said Elizabeth, pulling a face. But as he sat beside her she reached to draw him closer. 'Thank you, darling. Thank you for everything. And I'm sorry—truly I am.'

'Hush,' he breathed, kissing her willing lips. 'No more of that. We'll make a fresh start, beginning now.'

Misty-eyed, she watched as he unbuttoned his shirt, smiling at her with blue eyes that no longer held anything back.

'I love you, Jean-Michel,' she murmured, and when at last he came to her she finally tossed away her ideas about independence. It was much sweeter to be one of a pair.

We hope you have enjoyed this Large Print book. Other Chivers Press or Thorndike Press Large Print books are available at your library or directly from the publishers.

For more information about current and forthcoming titles, please call or write, without obligation, to:

Chivers Press Limited
Windsor Bridge Road
Bath BA2 3AX
England
Tel. (01225) 335336

OR

Thorndike Press
295 Kennedy Memorial Drive
Waterville
Maine 04901
USA

All our Large Print titles are designed for easy reading, and all our books are made to last.